# HENSHAW FIVE

# HENSHAW FIVE

## SHORT STORY COMPETITION WINNERS 2021–2023

## EDITED BY REBECCA COLLINS

This edition published in Great Britain in 2023

www.henshawpress.co.uk

Hobeck Books Limited, 24 Brookside Business Park, Stone, Staffordshire ST15 0RZ

www.hobeck.net



A CIP catalogue for this book is available from the British Library.

ISBN 978-1-915-817-19-8 (ebook)

ISBN 978-1-915-817-20-4 (pbk)

Cover design by Hobeck Books

*To all the writers in the world, big and small, tall and short, fact and fiction*

*AND*

*To all the young readers who attend the Christopher Whitehead Language College and Sixth Form, Worcester, UK*

# NOTES ON CONTRIBUTORS

## KIM BIGELOW

Kim Bigelow is a retired professor starting his fifth, or his sixth, career as a writer. He made his living writing media copy in Chicago for ten years, so strictly speaking this is his second writing career. Recently, his work was given the accolade Best Fiction of the Year by the *Saturday Evening Post*.

## DR DIANNE BOWN-WILSON

Dianne was born in England, grew up in New Zealand and now lives in Dartmoor National Park. She has a PhD in Organizational Behaviour. She writes character-led contemporary fiction – short stories and flash. Her work has either won prizes or been placed in numerous international competitions and included in several anthologies. Two collections of her successful stories have been published as: *Instructions for Living* (2017) nd *Degrees of Exposure* (2021). She is currently seeking representation for her first novel and working on the next.

## MARK BROUCEK

Mark started writing in earnest during lockdown in London, where you were only allowed out of your flat for one hour per day. To keep from watching 23 hours of Netflix daily, he got some ideas onto his iPad. Returning to the States, he has continued writing, though not as feverishly. If an idea keeps him up at night, he knows it's something he needs to write out. It's better than insomnia.

## STEVE BURFORD

Former English and drama teacher, Steve has written in a range of genres from Young Adult through romance to science fiction and horror. He is also the author of a series of police procedural novels: *It's A Sin* (2016), *Bodies Beautiful* (2018), *Sticks and Stones* (2021), *Crossed Lines* (2021), where the central male character is – honestly – not based on him, even if the central female character is based on one of his best friends.

## ANIL CLASSEN

Bookseller, blogger, writer, avid traveller, street food victim and dedicated follower of fashion, Anil Classen spent his first twenty-one years in the seaside city of Port Elizabeth, South Africa. He is a German writer of Indian descent living in Switzerland, with an academic background in Psychology,

English and Journalism. He divides his time between Zurich, Hamburg and Cape Town, each of these being called home at one stage of his life. At the moment, he is knee deep in meadow flowers in the countryside, working hard on his writing, this time a first draft for a potential novel.

## PETER COLLINS

Peter is a writer specialising in short stories. He has had some twenty stories published in hard copy anthologies and many more published online. His writing often features a quirky sense of humour and an unexpected twist. He has won a number of prizes for his writing and in 2021 was awarded the HG Wells Fiction Prize. He lives in Leeds, England and when not writing is often out in the Yorkshire countryside either cycling or walking his dog, Saski.

## PENNY DALE

Penny Dale (writing as Penny Rogers) writes mostly short stories, flash fiction and poetry. She has been published in print and online - including Henshaw Treats and Henshaw Two – and had some success in literary competitions. She is a member of the management team for SOUTH poetry magazine and facilitates a very informal writing group in her hometown.

## MARK DENZA

Mark writes short stories because he loves the challenge of condensing structure, plot and emotions into such a tight space. He is lucky enough to have been published in *Writers' forum*, *Writing* magazine, Henshaw Press, *Scribble* magazine, *Café Lit*, *The Manufacturers' Review*, Cranked Anvil, *Shorts* magazine and the Yeovil Literary Prize. He has just completed his first historical fiction novel.

Twitter: @markdemeza

## MARY FOX

After leaving a rock and roll career in accountancy, Mary decided to start a course in creative writing at City Lit in Holborn, London. Here, she was encouraged to write short stories. She has since been long- and short-listed in many competitions including The Bath Short Story Prize and The Wells Short Story Competition. Her stories have been published in UK anthologies including the Fish anthology, the GRIST anthology of protest, the *Momaya Short Story Review*. In the US, her stories have appeared in the Indignor House anthology, Stories through the Ages Babyboomers anthology and the Saints and Sinners LGBTQ+ literary festival anthology. She currently resides in Epsom with her husband, two children and a pair of hens named Tikka and Jalfrezi.

## VALERIE HOARE

Starting with a manual typewriter for Christmas at eleven years old, Valerie has written short fiction around retail work and then raising a family. There have been several successes in short story competitions over the years, though not as many as she would've liked. Some have even been published online and in anthologies. Often regretting her lack of further education, Valerie always hoped to return as a mature student, but life got in the way. She still feels there is more to come and, searching for wider spaces, she has completed two novels that are looking for homes and a third is in progress.

## RICHARD HOOTON

Born and brought up in Mansfield, Nottinghamshire, Richard Hooton studied English Literature at the University of Wolverhampton before becoming a journalist and communications officer. He has had numerous short stories published and has won prizes or been listed in various competitions. Richard lives in Mossley, near Manchester, and is a member of Mossley Writers.

## DON HORNE

Don never attempted to write fiction until a very mature age, after retiring his training consultancy. To that point, it was all business writing.  Short stories captured his interest, and he has received competition awards in Sydney, Melbourne and the UK.  He has now published two books – First, *Brady's Legacy* (2022) a romantic novella set at the outbreak of WW2, supported with a collection of short stories. Secondly, *Will Your Team Achieve Success?*, with common sense people skills for team leaders.

## SEÁN MCNICHOLL

Seán McNicholl is an Irish GP who enjoys writing short stories in a variety of genres. He has had work published in

*Beyond Words* literary magazine, *Raw Lit*, *34th Parallel*, *Bindweed*, and two anthologies from Wicked Shadow Press, among others. He has featured on the Blue Marble Storytellers podcast and the Read Lots Write Lots podcast.

www.seanmcnicholl.com

## DENARII PETERS

Denarii Peters was born in the northwest of England but now lives in the county of Lincolnshire. A former primary school teacher, she spends her days writing stories and drinking a lot of coffee. In the last year she has achieved longlist or better in 32 competitions across the world, including two third places, one second and one winning entry, which has resulted in twelve of her stories being or soon to be published in various anthologies, magazines and on websites. 'The Unkindness of Witches' was her first success.

## PAUL SHERMAN

Paul Sherman is a teacher, author and director of Youth Theatre. He has had numerous stories published in various hard copy magazines and online. He has had four horror novellas published. His collection of short stories, *Where Seagulls Dare* (2018), all set at different locations on the tiny channel island of Herm (steeped in history and mythology and ripe for short stories), was launched at the Guernsey Literary Festival in 2018, and the follow-up, *One Flew Over the Puffin's Nest*, will be launched in May this year. He also writes plays and his play set in the infamous Dublin Gaol, 'Kilmainham Kids', was premiered at the Barn Theatre, Milton

Keynes, a few years back. He has just completed a play ('Surpassing Strangeness') about the life of the surrealist photographer Claude Cahun (born Lucie Schwob in 1895), who together with her female partner launched their resistance campaign against the Germans during the occupation of Jersey in World War II. His love of Charles Dickens's *Great Expectations* is what led to the writing of 'Boy from the Bayou', which is loosely based on Dickens' story, but unfolds in steampunk style and is set in and around nineteenth-century New Orleans.

## BRYAN THOMAS

After affectations at twenty – the new Renaissance man – Bryan completed his architectural training and has run his own practice in northeast Essex for the last seventy years. He had always written poetry but decided to attend creative writing classes about twelve years ago (to keep ze little grey cells active). He has succeeded with short stories in numerous long and short lists with inclusions in anthologies. He has self-published two books of poetry, *Below the Shining* and *A Thermal of My Own*.

## RICHARD WESTWELL

Richard writes tales to read late at night in subtropical Australia, where he sits in the heat listening to the croak of cane toads and dreaming of his native London. His short stories have been published in various anthologies, including *Aesthetica* magazine's Creative Writing Award Annual, Fabula Press's *Aestas* collection and *Flash Fiction* magazine. Richard was long-listed for the Exeter Story Prize and shortlisted for the PulpFictional Flash Competition.

## VICTORIA DOWD (FOREWORD)

Victoria is a crime writer and author of the bestselling Smart Woman's mystery series. Her debut novel, *The Smart Woman's Guide to Murder*, won The People's Book Prize 2021 for fiction. It was also named In Search of the Classic Mystery's novel of the year. Victoria loves the short fiction form and was awarded the Gothic Fiction prize in 2019. Her work has been published in various literary journals and magazines. She has also appeared at various literary festivals, including Crimefest, Newcastle Noir, Crime in the Countryside and the International Agatha Christie Festival.

https://victoriadowd.com

## REBECCA COLLINS (EDITOR)

Rebecca is a published poet and contributed to *Because We Never Said Goodbye*, a collection of poems about Charlbury in Oxfordshire, published by Wychwood Press in 2008. She's also a ghost writer for Summersdale Publishing, the author of *The Best Mum Ever* (2017) and *The Best Dad Ever* (2017). She is the 'Beck' of Hobeck, alongside her partner in crime and everything else, Adrian Hobart, and is an aspiring artist.

# FOREWORD

Short stories can capture a single moment, a thought, an idea, so perfectly that it remains with the reader long after the final word. In the time it takes to drink a cup of tea, the reader can enter a new world and leave with something that will resonate throughout the rest of their day, perhaps longer. They are a concentrated art, a much more distilled form than the novel. It leaves the writer nowhere to hide.

Every word must earn its place. There is very little space to create that perfect alchemy of plot, character and setting. In only a few pages, the author must devise an entire arc that leaves the reader with a feeling of complete satisfaction at the end. It is a true test of the ability of a writer to enthral the reader, often in only a few hundred words, and maintain that intense connection for those few stolen moments in a day. The stories in this anthology unhook the reader from the real world in a variety of intriguing and nuanced ways.

There are the seemingly inconsequential moments of life, such as a child's song, leaving the reader to reflect on issues that linger long after the melody has ended. A man's visit to an old schoolteacher creates an enduring sense of melancholy and disempowerment. An aching sense of loss remains for the woman who has spent years waiting for the love to return who never will.

The minutiae of life in all its beauty and sadness is captured in these tiny glimpses of existence. It is, as with all great short story anthologies, a vast kaleidoscope of emotions ranging over a multitude of experiences from the smallest of moments to the huge and overwhelming parts of life. Love is found and lost for a mother who has embarked on a relationship that could never end well. The simple act of growing a rose is as powerful and affecting as an account of how a daughter's death results from a TV show. The nature of our identity and regrets flow from a chance meeting. We find unadulterated horror when a letter is read by lantern light.

These stories, although so different in subject, character and style, all have one thread running through them. They capture the essence of an emotion and pin it down with such clarity and keen observation that the reader is utterly immersed in that person's existence for the short time they have with them.

However, it is not just the quality of each story that makes an anthology work as a whole. Unlike the novel, people will read these stories in a variety of ways. Some do read the stories in order, choosing to follow the editor's often agonizing choice of where each story should sit. Others dip in and out of an anthology, perhaps alongside reading many different books. In some ways, it offers the reader an opportunity to re-arrange the anthology and decide which story attracts them at that point. Often this choice rests on nothing more than a captivating title or perhaps a familiar author.

Yet, however the reader chooses to engage with the anthology, by some almost unfathomable magic, the substance of it remains. There were many entries for this competition. The end result not only contains individual stories which stand alone as works of immense talent but also come together as a whole, creating a narrative that flows beneath the entirety of the anthology. This is a real treat for the short story lover, encompassing sweeps of emotion and fleeting moments that linger delicately. By the end, it leaves the reader with a lasting sense of fulfilment and many questions, the primary one being, can we have more?

Victoria Dowd, *June 2023*

# CONTENTS

# PORCH LIGHT

## KIM BIGELOW

*A porch light always says, 'Welcome Home'*

The Sheriff Traynor tipped his hat. "Good evening, Miss Mira. This here is Mr. Tom August. He's from one of them big newspapers back East. He's writin' 'bout people livin' in a small town. I just brought him by to say hi." The Sheriff held out a cake box. "Anna made a cake this morning and wanted you to have it."

Miss Mira smiled as we came onto the porch. "Well, thank you kindly, Sheriff. Seems like everybody's droppin' by today with a pie or casserole or some such thing. I swear Michael is gonna get fatter than that lazy ole rooster of mine." She held out her hand to be shaken. "Pleased to meet you, Mr. August." She turned on the porch light that started flickering like a trapped moth. Mira turned back to us. "Michael told me to keep the light on so he can find his way home."

Sheriff Traynor took off his hat as we came into the house. "You all sit anywhere you like," said Mira, "I'll just make us some lemonade and then Mr. August can tell me all about himself." Mira headed to the kitchen to cut up some lemons. The Sheriff called toward the kitchen. "Your porch light needs fixin', Miss Mira."

"I know, Sheriff, but Michael's comin' home tomorrow. I'll get him to fix it."

"I could send one of the boys over. Michael will surely have better things to do than climb up and down ladders."

"That's kind of you, Sheriff." Mira came into the parlor with a frosted glass pitcher, slices of lemon floating on top. She put the tray down and poured the lemonade into three tall glasses. The ice cubes crackled as if they were happy to be free of the large chunk she kept stored in an old style ice box.

"So, Mr. August, where are you from?" Mira asked.

"New York, ma'am, born and bred."

"And you want to write about our quaint little town?"

"I'm doing a piece on lost traditions, ma'am. How some good things people do get forgotten over time."

"Well, that's a fine thing," she said. "You come back tomorrow and talk to Michael. He'll give you an earful. Been just about everywhere, I reckon."

"That's a fine idea, Miss Mira, we'll do that," said the Sheriff.

We stayed half an hour and then the Sheriff stood up. "Well, time we was goin'. You say hi to Michael for me."

"I surely will, Sheriff. It was nice of you to stop by."

As we got into the cruiser I said, "Thanks, Sheriff. Miss Mira is what I always thought a true gentlewoman of the South would be like."

"That she is." The Sheriff didn't start the car, just stared at the keys. "You're probably wonderin' why I brought you all the way out here?"

"Not at all," I said. "I enjoyed meeting her."

"I'm gonna tell you a story," he said, "won't take long."

"This have to do with living in a small town?" I asked

"It has everything to do with everything," he said.

I took out a notebook.

"Don't write none of this down. You'll remember it, but you got to promise not to print none of this till I say."

In my line of work, you hear a lot of 'off the record' stories. I put the pencil away and the Sheriff started telling his story: "This happened nigh on fifty years ago; right after the government set up the lottery that sent all them poor boys to Vietnam to get killed." The Sheriff shook his head. "I still can't imagine makin' boys go someplace they never even heard of, so they could fight to protect a corrupt government that all the people hated. I was exempt on account of bein' in law enforcement. I was just a Deputy, dumb as a twig on a tree. This was way back when Mitch Singleton was Sheriff. I was doin' my rounds one night when I found Michael Finnerty hanging upside down from a tree. Been cut maybe fifty times. No one cut would have done him much harm, but with so many cuts, he'd almost bled out. There was a sign pinned to his chest sayin' this is what happened to Commies and deserters. I cut him down and leaned him against the tree. Knew he wasn't gonna last long, so I took out a recorder and had him tell me who done this, what they said, every-thing that happened. He died five minutes later. That recording is what's called a dying man's declaration. Not hardly any stronger evidence in a court of law. Buried that poor boy right under that big ol' tree and went to look for the boys who done it. Walked into Joe's Bar, but stayed in the back listenin' to Ronnie Quirrel braggin'.

"'Funniest thing you ever saw.' Ronnie was swiggin' beer like they was gonna quit makin' it. 'Hoowee.' He held up the beer. 'You shoulda seen that boy cryin' and beggin', but that didn't matter none to me. I promise he and none of them other college boys gonna ever come down here, botherin' our women, tellin' us how we should all march on Washington to protest the war. That boy kept sayin' he was on his way to Canada. Goin' there to avoid the draft, the coward.'

"One of the other drinkers nodded and said, 'Your country calls, you gotta go. End of story.'

"Ronnie nodded his head and downed another shot, followed by more beer. 'Damn straight. We can't be havin' any of them people come down here spoutin' their anti-segregation, anti-war bullshit.'

"I walked out of the bar and waited. Hit Ronnie over the head as he was staggerin' toward his car, dragged him to my truck and drove to Hill's Canyon. Asked him a few questions, then threw him over the edge like he was common trash. Knew there wouldn't be much left of him in a couple of weeks. Then I went and got any of the boys had anythin' to do with the hangin' and drove 'em back to the canyon. Handcuffed 'em to the cruiser and to each other. Told 'em I'd already throwed Ronnie into the canyon and they was next.

"'It was all Ronnie,' they was all cryin'. Said they was drinkin' and didn't know what Ronnie had in mind, till he blocked the road and dragged poor Michael out of his car and tied him up. Threw a rope over the tree and hauled him up like a piece of meat. They tol' me how Ronnie took out a knife and started cuttin' on Michael; made cuts all over his body. Then he turned and give the knife to each one of them boys an' said they could cut Michael or join him on the next branch.

"Stupid kids. What was I gonna do? Destroy the lives of them four boys? Tol' 'em I could shoot 'em right where they stood and pitch them into Hill's Canyon for the buzzards and coyotes to chew on, or they could do the right thing. Tol' 'em Mira was supposed to marry that boy when the war was finished and he was free to come back. Only now he weren't never comin' back and that was gonna just about break that poor girl's heart.

"Bobby Taylor tol' me he was right sorry. Said he didn't mean for none of it to happen, that he liked Michael. 'You tell me what to do,' he said, 'and I'll do it.'

"I played the tape for them, turned the volume up right loud so they could hear Michael say all their names. 'I play this in front of a Federal Judge and none of you is ever gonna see the outside of a jail cell the rest of your lives. That or get hanged,' I said.

"The rest of them boys said they'd do whatever I tol' 'em to do.

"'You all are gonna stay here in Fremont and take care of Miss Mira the rest of her days. She got a field needs plowin' or a cow needs milkin', you're gonna see it gets done. An' you ain't never gonna tell nobody what happened. She'd do herself an injury if she knew. I hear anyone in town say anything, I play the tape. Any of you leave town, I play the tape. You understand?'

"They nodded their heads and that's the way it's been for the last fifty odd years."

"But Sheriff," I said, "I heard Miss Mira say Michael was coming back."

"Jimmy Carter pardoned all them boys that went to Canada on January 21, 1977. Tol' 'em to come back home."

I nodded. "And tomorrow's the twenty-second, the day Michael would have come back all those years ago."

"Most days Miss Mirabelle is just as sweet and pleasant as anybody I know. Ever'one in town is kind to her, treats her like a lady, which she is. But once a year, she dresses herself up and turns on the porch light, waitin' for Michael to come home."

"Like a candle in the window," I said. "So Sheriff, why are you telling me all this?"

"I got a cancer," he said. "Won't be around much longer. After Miss Mira passes, you can tell the story."

"No one will believe me without the tape."

"I'll leave you the tape," said Traynor. "I just want people to know what happened to that poor boy. You're a reporter. You're all the memory some people will ever have, so that's what I want you to do, be their memory."

"Okay, Sheriff," I said, "I can do that."

Years later, I moved back to that little town, settled down and started a family. The Sheriff, Mira and the four boys were all gone by then. I wrote the story, but never printed it. Like the Sheriff, I didn't see the sense in ruining the memories the townfolk had of all those people. I don't know. Maybe someone else will print the story after I'm gone. Still, I make it a habit, once a year, in January, to go outside and turn the porch light on. Keep it on all night to remind me of a sweet Southern woman waiting for her Michael to come home.

# THE MAN-FRIEND

## DIANNE BOWN-WILSON

My daughter, Lauren, just called. One of *The Sisterhood* (as she calls her unattached girlfriends) wants her to go out for drinks tonight.

'Will you babysit?' she asked, more a demand than a request.

I had to tell her I couldn't.

'Why not? Don't tell me you've got something better to do.' Immediately her tone was sharp-edged, only half-joking.

I picked up on this because I know her inside-out. What she was thinking was: *What's the point of a mother if you can't rely on them to drop everything and come and look after your kids?*

'Actually, I have. I'm meeting up with a friend. It's been arranged for ages; I'm sure I mentioned it.'

'I don't think so. Anyway, who? Someone I know?'

'No. From work – way back.'

'Man or woman?'

I started to panic. 'Oh, for goodness sakes. A man, actually.

But he's just an old colleague. Anyway, I have to go now; I'll tell you about it tomorrow.'

'Fine.'

It wasn't fine. It was a lie as subtle as over-ripe cheese. But I hadn't anticipated her call, and didn't have an oven-ready alibi. There's no way I could have told her the truth.

Tonight's the ninth time he and I will be meeting up; I know the number exactly. I've managed to keep these meetings secret until now, but after this conversation, I feel my luck might be running out. I push the thought away. I know Lauren would love me to be going on 'a date' – she's been nagging me for ages to 'get out there', but although it's been three years since Alan died, it still feels too soon. Besides, as I function within a Bermuda Triangle bordered by my part-time bookkeeping job, child-minding for Lauren, and helping take a group of pensioners supermarket shopping, I'm hardly likely to stumble across any eligible men. So no, this friendship isn't about dating.

———

Once again, I drive myself to the pub, a small place in a village back street some twenty miles away from where I live. It's hardly stylish, certainly not one of those glitzy gastro-pubs that Lauren favours, but it's a good place for a quiet midweek chat and a bite of something – the sort of under-stated atmosphere we like.

When I arrive, he's already there, sitting sideways on a stool at the bar, keeping an eye on the door. He sees me and grins, then pecks me on the cheek. 'Good to see you!' While he orders me a glass of wine, I go and bag our usual table in the corner.

I haven't seen him for a couple of weeks, but he looks okay. Tired – but who isn't these days? He works long hours and, on top of that, has a lot on his plate: children, his parents, financial problems. But his opening words circumvent all of this. 'So, what did you think of the book?'

I don't need to question what he means. Last time we met, we ended up having a lively debate about Margaret Atwood and Bernadine Evaristo and the merits of the Booker Prize. He'd read both books, whereas I hadn't started Bernadine's, and he made me promise I would.

'Fabulous, I loved it. Thanks for pushing me. What are you reading now?'

'Probably nothing I can persuade you to take on. I've plunged into sci-fi lately – pure escapism, but it works for me.'

I pull a face, and he laughs, knowing I loathe black holes and cyborgs.

This is why I love our meetings: our conversations, discussing topics that usually remain submerged in the mire of everyday life. He's a thinker, but not an intellectual, just an ordinary working person like me. The interests we share are eclectic but commonplace: reading, films, philosophy, art – and we both love a good laugh. I treasure our friendship, knowing that romance and the complexities of a physical relationship will never rear their intrusive heads.

We first arranged to meet up after I'd asked him, as we chatted on the phone, whether he could think of anything that might cheer him up and make his life more tolerable. He didn't take long to answer. 'You know what, I'd love to go out with someone to have a meal and a conversation – not about anything specific but just to remind myself that I'm still a fully-functioning, normal human being.'

'Mmm, I know what you mean. Most of my female friends either have husbands or partners they feel they have to include, or they want to turn 'meeting up' into a group event. It all gets to be a bit much.'

It's one of the things I miss most about Alan. As well as my husband, he was my best friend, and we'd often go out for a meal and spend the evening talking about nothing very much. 'The sort of things that cross your mind but aren't worth making space for,' was how he put it. But I didn't say anything about that to my friend because although he and I chat about just about anything, very little of it is personal. Sometimes we discuss his children, but not his marriage. I say nothing about how mine was or my relationship with Lauren. And we try not to speak about the obvious, which is that we have to keep our relationship hidden, whereas Alan and I were free to go anywhere we pleased.

Lauren, as predicted, is now mad keen to know more. First thing this morning, she texted me: *So how was your *date*?????*

*Fine. No date – we were just catching up.*

Lauren knows all about dating. In my opinion, she launched into it with indecent haste when she split with Dan six months ago. I said as much to my sister, Janet, at the time.

'She's young still,' Janet said. 'Perhaps she's still trying to establish her identity outside of being a mother and, until now, a wife. It's hard, as we both know.'

'Hmm. You didn't rush out and start dating when you left Brian,' I reminded her.

She laughs. 'No. But who knows – perhaps I would have done if Tinder had been around! Things change, Gill. Perhaps she needs to spread her wings. As long as the children are okay, does it really matter?'

Well, yes, it matters to me.

The real reason Lauren's dating rankles with me is that I think she behaved badly during her marriage and was totally unjustified in asking Dan to leave. When she dropped the bombshell that they were splitting up, my obvious response was, 'Why – what's happened?' But there seemed to be no particular reason. 'Oh, he's just a total waste of space,' she sighed. 'Spending time with him is about as exciting as watching paint dry.'

"So why did you marry him?' I wanted to say.

But I didn't, because I know why.

She married him because having a big fancy wedding was the thing to do. And then she had babies for the same reason. I'd never reveal this to anyone, not even Janet, but the way my daughter's view of the world starts and stops with herself horrifies me. She's my child, and I love her to bits, yet in some ways, she's a stranger. Frankly, in terms of how she treated Dan, I'm ashamed of how she's turned out. It's the main reason I look after her children. If she's out there confronting the real world, I hope she might eventually grow up and adopt a less selfish approach. *And* have less energy for dating.

So far, my strategy doesn't seem to have been working.

As I was in the office today, Lauren didn't call me until this evening. When she did, she went straight for the kill. 'So what did you do last night? Where did you go? Who *is* this person?'

This time I was ready for her and appalled myself by how easily I lied about my fictitious ex-colleague-and-his-wife-and-grown-children-and-how-we-went-to-the-pub-by-the-river-and-had-steak-and-chips-and-red-wine. 'Back home by 9.30,' I laughed. 'Hardly a wild night out.'

'And will you be seeing him again?'

'Unlikely. He lives up north now and was only here for his father's funeral.'

'Oh.' It seems she believes me.

'And you? Did you find someone to babysit so you could go out?'

'No. Actually, I didn't try. I decided I'd rather stay at home and watch TV.'

'Not like you...'

'Mmm, I think I'm getting too old for partying. Much as I hate to say it, I even miss Dan.'

'That's a first.'

For a moment, there was silence on the line. 'Not really,' she said wistfully. 'You know, I've been thinking a lot lately. I might park the divorce idea for a while. The kids miss him, and he did have his good points.'

'Oh?'

'I've realised how much I used to like talking to him; he was a great listener. And he could always make me laugh. Perhaps it might be an idea to have another go.'

'Would he want to come back?'

'Maybe not. I have treated him pretty badly, so I can't just whistle for him like he's a dog. Not that I'd want that anyway.'

'No.'

I hear her sigh softly. 'But would you say there's hope, Mum?'

'There's always hope.'

I say nothing more. Whether and however Lauren wants to work towards a reunion is nothing to do with me. She's an adult and needs to reach her own conclusions. I don't even know if I think it's a good thing because although reconciliation would carry plenty of pluses for Lauren and the kids, I feel Dan deserves much more.

———

Our next get-together was planned for next Thursday night, but just now, I phoned to tell him it's all off. As he didn't answer, I left a message, breathing deeply to control my emotions: 'I'm sorry. Meeting up with you has been great, but we both know it's probably unwise. I think for everyone's sakes, we should stop now.'

I put down the phone, biting back tears. As a woman, it's hard to have a man-friend.

It's impossible when he's your son-in-law, and you know he'll soon be going back to his wife.

# REDHEAD REUNION

## DIANNE BOWN-WILSON

'Hey, it is you, isn't it?'

Carole's daydreaming in the queue at the Tesco Express next to the station when she feels a light touch on her shoulder. She spins around, and her eyes connect with a tall, grey-haired man about her own age, grinning like he's won the lottery.

She raises an eyebrow, unsure of how to respond.

'It's Gareth from Uni, 1989's greatest dancer! Remember?'

She smiles uncertainly, but he seems unfazed by her lack of recognition.

'Well, okay, I guess I have changed a bit,' he laughs. 'Gained a few pounds and lost a few hairs. But you – the moment I glanced across, I just knew it had to be.'

'Heavens.'

'Truth told, I don't know that I would have recognised your face after all this time, despite your lovely blue eyes and freckles. But those amazing auburn curls...' He shakes his head, and she raises her hand and touches her hair lightly as if wary of its power.

'Do you remember how I used to tell you you'd never get away with committing a crime with hair as memorable as that? And here's the proof, I spotted you immediately.' He laughs again.

She nods in acknowledgement, smiling vaguely – as you do when you've just been yanked out of your reverie and are struggling to reconnect with reality. It's something she frequently experiences these days. *To be expected*, she's been told.

'Look, I can see you're lost for words right now, and you're just about to go through the checkout. So why don't I wait for you outside, and we'll chat then?' He gestures towards the door. 'I'm desperate to hear all your news.'

'Oh, okay,' she says slowly, back-footed and not knowing how to refuse. 'I'll see you there.'

———

A few minutes later, she exits the store and sees him at once despite wondering if she'd recognise him in the busy street. A canvas satchel hangs from his shoulder, but his hands are empty, while she now carries two bulging carrier bags full of provisions for the weekend. 'All done?' he asks.

'Sure,' she says. 'But don't you have any shopping?'

'No. I only popped in to get a sandwich to take on the train home; you can never be sure if they'll have anything.'

'Home? Where's that?'

'Same as ever, Newcastle. But it looks like you stayed on here after Uni. Is it a good place to live?'

She nods slowly. 'The city's changed a lot recently, but it's still a really vibrant place.'

'Sure is. Not that I'm here often—' His words are drowned out by the roar of a passing motorbike. As she turns her head away, she's jostled by a group of passers-by and recoils from the contact.

'Not the best place to talk,' she says, fighting back rising panic. This is the first time in weeks she's been out by herself; all of a sudden, it's a bit overwhelming.

'No.' He frowns. 'Look, I realise you're probably busy, but do you have time for a quick coffee? I feel it has to be fate coming across you after all these years, and I'd love to hear how your life's turned out.'

'Um...'

'Please, I know I don't deserve it after how things ended, but it really would mean a lot to me.' Now anxiety clouds his green eyes as though the demons of his past have risen to confront him. He glances around and nods in the direction of a cafe. 'That place over there looks okay.'

She takes a deep breath. Should she? Why not? Before she came out, she told herself she had to be bold, and really, what could go wrong?

He moves a couple of paces toward the café. 'Anyway, my train leaves in forty minutes, so you don't have to worry you'll be stuck with me.' His pleading gives him a look of vulnerability, which momentarily tugs at her heart.

'Sure, let's go,' she says.

Service is frustratingly slow inside the coffee shop, but at least it's warm, and they can speak without shouting. He's volunteered to buy the coffee, so she sits at a table, observing him in the queue at the counter. He's lean and tanned, still in good shape for his years. He would have been a heartbreaker when he was young.

When he finally joins her, he wastes no time on niceties. 'There's so much I want to ask you. But first, I want to say how deeply sorry I am for what I did. I was an unbelievable bastard.'

'Oh.'

He looks into her eyes as if expecting her to say more, but she sits impassively, hands folded in her lap, waiting for him to continue.

'To say it was the ignorance and stupidity of youth isn't entirely true. I was a self-centred little shit who was incapable of caring about anyone but myself. To be honest, looking back, I don't know what you saw in me.'

He searches her face, eyes beseeching her for a reaction.

She remains aloof.

'When you told me you were pregnant, I felt I'd been handed a death sentence. All I could think of was to run. Did you know I went abroad?'

She shakes her head slowly.

'My parents thought it was the right thing to do, which I can see now says a lot about them. They gave me some money and arranged for me to disappear when what they should have done was make me face up to my actions.' He shakes his head. 'Great parenting, eh? Anyway, no one except them knew where I was, which is why you were never able to track me down. I assume you tried because although nothing was said at the time, my mother admitted before she passed away that they'd received some letters from you and destroyed them rather than passing them on.'

'I see.' Carole nods gravely as if this news confirms her

suspicions. The scenario's straight out of a Victorian melo-drama, even though it was only a few decades ago.

'I only came back from Australia recently when she died. I didn't have to, but something beckoned, some feeling that I needed to start putting matters right.'

He's been torturing himself over this for a long time, Carole thinks. He needs to get it off his chest. But she says nothing.

'You'll possibly be pleased to know that following that auspicious start, I made a complete mess of my life. Three marriages, three divorces, two children who won't speak to me, and a bankrupt business due to my mismanagement.' He laughs bitterly. 'God – divine justice, or what? Except that it wasn't; it was me. It took me until I turned fifty to finally accept that everything that had happened wasn't due to bad luck and fate but my own incompetence and misplaced sense of importance.' He sighs deeply, his eyes now fixed on the tabletop.

At last, she responds. 'At least you've had that insight, regardless of how accurate it might be.'

'Oh, it's true, all right. And hopefully, back then, you came to the same conclusion about what I was like and didn't blame yourself for me leaving you.'

She looks at him with a steady gaze. 'What happened was a long time ago.'

They sit in silence for a moment, dwelling on all that's hiding behind his words, until eventually, she continues. 'If it helps, I believe that looking back on your life can be a good thing if it makes you resolve to do things differently and try to be a better person. Recently, I've been through the same process myself. What I concluded is that if you've still got some time left, you've still got the opportunity to do some good in the world, regardless of the past. And if you don't seize that opportunity, forgive yourself, and move on, then life isn't worth living. Perhaps, in the end, your mother decided to do some good by telling you about those letters?'

He nods, apparently deep in thought. 'Possibly.'

Suddenly, he glances at his watch. 'Oh my God, look at the time! I have to go, and I haven't asked you anything about yourself. What happened after I abandoned you? Did you have the baby? Are you married? Have you had a happy life?' His questions gush forth as if from an unblocked drain.

She shakes her head. Where would she start? Marriage, miscarriages, alcohol abuse, affairs, divorce... So much to regret. 'There's no time for all that, I'm afraid.'

'But I need to know I didn't ruin your life. Please tell me I didn't.'

She smiles. 'You couldn't. As I think you've realised, everyone's life is their responsibility. How mine turned out is down to me.'

'But—'

She holds up a hand. 'You'll miss your train.'

'Can we stay in touch? Already I feel so much better for speaking to you, but I need some more answers.'

'It wouldn't be a good idea.'

'Just give me your phone number so we can talk once more. Just once – then I promise I'll leave you alone. Please, I beg you.'

'Okay.' She can't risk him staying any longer, so when he hands her his phone, she punches in a number – two digits different from her own – and quickly hands it back.

'Thank you; this means so much.'

She smiles woodenly. She feels she should respond more warmly and find some additional words of encouragement, but with mere seconds remaining, what good would it do?

Her last view of him is at the coffee shop door as he turns back to her and mouths 'Goodbye', raising a hand in farewell.

————

Later, back home at her flat, Carole collapses onto the sofa and kicks off her shoes. Her older sister, Rachel, her live-in companion since her diagnosis, appears in the doorway.

'Hi, I thought I heard a taxi,' she says. 'Is everything okay?'

'Yep, all good, though I have to say I'm exhausted now.'

'So, how was it? Did you enjoy your outing?'

'Sure. The city centre was a bit overwhelming after so long away, but otherwise, it was fine. I went in, negotiated the crowds, and emerged unscathed. I even did the shopping. So now I feel I can say with absolute conviction that I've joined the ranks of chemo survivors. Henceforth life will go on!'

Her sister laughs. 'Good on you. It's brave of you to get back on track; I'm proud of your determination.'

Carole shrugs. 'It's good—all good. But I think I'll take it easy for the next few days.' As she speaks, she reaches up and tugs at her hairline, peeling away the auburn wig. 'I'm so glad to get this off, though. Itchy and hot just don't describe it, although it's still better than being bald.'

'Yeah, but what a look you've chosen: carroty curls – Orphan Annie, eat your heart out!'

Carole laughs. 'It seemed a good excuse to try out being

an entirely different person. And you know what, while I was out, I met the strangest guy who was totally convinced he knew me...'

# I'LL DO ANYTHING

MARK BROUCEK

Jack Meyers was sitting in total darkness, as he always did at the start of the show. It was much better theatre for the contestants to be hidden from the audience until that exact moment when the announcer called out their names. Then a spotlight would hit them and the world would see a startled, and momentarily blinded, man or woman with nothing to lose. The combination of shock, nervousness, and false hope created a look that the producers banked on every week – and was always delivered.

As three-time returning champion, Jack should have been prepared for the spot. But he never was and he gave the producers exactly what they wanted. He hated them, and himself, for that.

Jack was particularly on edge tonight. Since he was back for a fourth week in a row, he had to come up with something even more spectacular than last week. And he really *was* back for a fourth week. Unlike most game shows, which taped up to five shows a day to be replayed during the coming weeks,

Jack's was live. While this was done to heighten the tension, it played havoc with Jack's nerves and ulcers during the wait between shows.

As the sweat literally dripped from his armpits to his waistband, Jack listened to the familiar fake enthusiasm of host Bob Sindelar:

"Hello everybody and welcome back to beautiful downtown Burbank, California! Thanks for joining us for another episode of the most intense and nerve-wracking hour on television!! We do what no one else dares to! And it's all LIVE! So, without further ado, let's play, *I'll Do Anything!* (pause for applause) Let's meet our contestants! First, this week's challenger: He's a dock worker from right down the road in Inglewood, meet Randall Brackin!!" The spot hit Brackin full on and he smiled queasily. "What are you willing to do for us tonight?" squealed Sindelar.

"Well, Bob," said Brackin, squinting and shading his eyes, "I'm gonna go over to my boss's Man of the Year award ceremony, rush the stage and confront him with pictures I took of him with the prostitute I set him up with." The audience cheered wildly and Sindelar had to shush them to have his velvet tones heard.

"Well, I'm guessing that you don't really need your job! Am I right, Randall?"

"Actually, Bob, I do," said Brackin. "My wife is eight months pregnant, my kids need braces and Mom just had a stroke and moved in with us. But for this show, I'll Do Anything!!" The crowd erupted again. Sindelar shushed again.

"Well, that's going to be tough to beat! But now, we move to our three time defending champion, from Van Nuys – Jack

Meyers!" The applause was good but not what Jack had been hoping for. The crowd seemed to be taken with this Brackin guy and that really concerned him. He'd have to come up with something pretty good. The sweat continued to pour. "What have you got for us tonight, Jack?" burst out Sindelar.

Jack sneaked a peek over at his opponent. The look in Brackin's eyes convinced Jack that he would go through with his stunt and not chicken out like others had. He had to come up with *something*. He looked back into the spotlight and, seeing nothing, said, "I'll kill my own daughter." The studio went absolutely silent. Then all hell broke loose.

*I'll Do Anything* was the brainchild of Sindelar-Maxwell Productions. After years of great, but not immense, pay as a game show host, Bob Sindelar (nee Walter Kandelterry) realized that for him to achieve the respect, and money, that he deserved, he needed to start his own production company. In the beginning, there were quite a few false starts. The most memorable, *Running On Empty*, was a show in which opponents answered progressively *easier* questions over a five day period – the catch being they could not eat or sleep during that time. The last coherent answer was the winner. Finally, Sindelar-Maxwell pitched the concept of *I'll Do Anything* to ABC Daytime.

Since there actually was no Maxwell (Sindelar had noticed that most successful game show production companies were collaborations, so he just made one up), Sindelar went it alone. This time he hit pay dirt. The idea was relatively simple. Each week, two contestants would make a statement about what they were willing to do for that week's prize money. Then they had to do it.

What made ABC bite was Sindelar's two unalterable tenets to the show. First, there had to be consequences to the contestant's actions. No "I'm gonna cuss out my boss to win the money and then let him know later on it was a joke – ha ha" would be allowed. The statements had to be serious and real. Try to tell the LAPD that the bank robbery you just attempted was a joke for TV – ha ha. If you wanted to be on *I'll Do Anything*, you had to be ready to lay it all on the line.

Second, the show had to be live. This was for two reasons. Sindelar had seen too many reality shows where the editing had made sympathetic characters into villains and vice versa. He wanted his contestants to be who they were, warts and all. The other reason had to do in part with his philosophy of laying it all out. With intros, credits and Sindelar's speeches, opponents had a maximum of 41 minutes to complete their challenges. There was no time to pussy foot around. You jumped in and did what you said you would do or you didn't and were humiliated in front of millions.

After the show had been greenlit, Sindelar had an epiphany of such monumental proportions that it virtually guaranteed a ratings monster: the prize money. The other reality shows were falling all over each other trying to give out the biggest prize each week. One was touting a chance at a $1 million payday for a night's trivia work. Hell, a mediocre *Jeopardy* payout was $25 – 30 grand and that was assured to the day's winner. Sindelar wanted his prize money to be so nominal that people watching could not believe that these schlubs would attempt such things for so little cash. The "I can't stop watching this train wreck" factor would be through the roof. He started out with a $1,000 for the first week's winner, then progressively 2, 3, and 5 grand in the coming weeks if you kept winning. You were retired after a four week stay as champion.

The network expressed doubt that people would stand for such minimal winnings. Sindelar held fast and was right. With all the nuts in California, he had to beat prospective contestants off with a two by four before selecting the right sad sack for any given show. Why give a million when they would have settled for $50, just to get on TV. And all the more profit for Sindelar-Maxwell Productions.

The show was successful beyond anyone's wildest dreams. It was moved to primetime and Sindelar and ABC couldn't even begin to count all the cash that was rolling in. Until May 21st that is, and Jack Meyers' five little words.

———

Jack knew he was in trouble. He was sitting in the show's Green Room, which had been turned into the Interrogation Room. He should have known that a show seen live across the entire country would be seen by the Burbank Police Dept. Officers arrived at the studio before the audience was even brought to order. They shut down the show immediately. He wondered what reruns were being shown on ABC right now. He didn't have the guts to flick on the room's TV so he just waited for another round of cops to drop by.

The door finally opened and in walked Sindelar followed by two men Jack didn't recognize. Detectives probably. "Jack, Jack, Jack," sighed Sindelar. He wasn't as enthusiastic sounding as he was on air but was just as condescending.

"The show's lawyers and I have gone over your story with a fine tooth comb and we think it's a go. But you gotta tell these guys one more time."

Jack couldn't believe his ears. It's a go? What's a go? Him to jail or the show continuing on? He was thinking he might be having some sort of a breakdown when Sindelar prompted him. "Just tell your story, Jack. Then we'll go back to the studio."

Unless they were going back to the studio to televise his trial and execution (which Jack didn't fully put past Sindelar), he wasn't getting arrested. He began his story. "My life was normal four years ago. Wife, two kids, dog, crappy job. Just like every other American, right? Then Marie, my youngest, runs right out in front of an ice cream truck. Can you believe it? Those things move so slow, you could walk faster. But Marie got tangled up underneath it and to this day is still on life support."

He paused, thinking about so many things. "She's not coming back," he finally said, "and the insurance is gone. We have no money. Dr. Wilson advised us to consider pulling the plug, if we were strong enough. We're not. Until I cracked and said what I said. My wife, Ellen, can't go on watching Marie fade. I guess I thought I could use the show to make me do what I know I have to." He looked around at everyone in the room and added, "That's it. End of story."

No one spoke. Finally, the two detectives sighed, shrugged and left the room. Sindelar sprang into action. "Okay, Jack here's what has to go down to keep us all out of a courtroom. We go back into the studio and you repeat what you're going to do. Tell your story." He thought for a moment. "Some tears would be good. Yeah. And then we go do it. We'll have to break into the news in some markets but who cares. This is big."

"What about Brackin?" Jack asked.

"Screw him," said Sindelar. "He can't beat you no matter what. Besides that Man of the Year dinner is probably over by now."

"Then what?" asked Jack.

"Then what what?"

"What happens next?"

"Oh," said Sindelar. "Well, you get the five grand and retire as four-time champ. And the show ends with its greatest champion ever."

Jack just looked at him. "The show goes off the air?"

"Well, that's what we worked out with ABC and the FCC. You know, it's for the best all the way around. I mean, who could beat you. You're the winner of all time."

Jack thought about it a bit. "So, the show goes off the air," he finally said.

"Yes, yes," said Sindelar impatiently. "It goes off the air. So, are we going or not?"

"Sure," said Jack. "Let's do it." They went into the studio, calmed the audience (who had the foresight to stick around, sensing that the show must go on) and reiterated Jack's earlier statement. Then, with camera crew in tow, they went off to Cedars-Sinai Medical Center to fulfill his pledge.

# SLOW LEARNER

## STEVE BURFORD

"Mr. Simms? It is you, isn't it? Hello, Sir."

"Er, hi." Terry Simms shook the hand held out to him but didn't get up from his desk. This after-school visitor to his classroom looked too young to be a parent, and definitely too scruffy to be an inspector or someone important.

"You don't remember me, do you?"

Terry groaned inwardly, understanding now what he was dealing with. Why did ex-students on nostalgia trips always choose the worst times to revisit their old schools? "I thought I recognised the face," he lied. "You'll have to forgive me though. I've got a terrible head for names."

"No worries! Years ago now. Time flies. That's a cliché that, isn't it?"

"Yes, but—"

"You always said we'd forget everything five minutes after we left school, but I remembered that, about clichés."

Terry forced a smile. "Well, that's grand, but you really

will have to forgive me, Mr…?" The deliberate formality of 'Mr' hung heavy but unanswered in the air.

The young man laughed. "Yeah, you always got our names wrong, back in the day. Course, we made it trickier for you, giving you wrong ones, answering for mates when you called the register, that kind of thing." He held up his hands. "Nothing personal. We did it to all the new teachers."

*New.* Terry had been at Monastery Grove for twelve years, so this man had to be…

"Remember Geoff Young?"

"You're Geoff?" The name stirred memories, but somehow still didn't seem right.

"Spencer Matthews? Neil Hyatt? Paul Harding?"

Terry snapped his fingers. "5E!"

"5F."

In spite of himself, Terry half-smiled. The very first Year Eleven class he'd taught. The kids from hell he'd thought he'd never forget. "There was Jonathan wasn't there? And Darren, and…"

"That's me!"

"Darren Richards?"

"Darren Taylor."

"Of course." Terry tried but couldn't summon up the face of the younger Darren. "Are you still in touch with the others?"

Taking this for the invitation it wasn't, Darren sat down at the desk in front of Terry's. "Spencer joined the navy. Neil works down the Box with his Dad. Paul buggered off to London. And Geoff Young," he shrugged, "went down for ten years last month."

Terry gave a rueful laugh. "A wide variety of life experiences. Thanks for bringing me up to date." He reached out his hand again. "Well, it's been good to see you, but I'm afraid now—"

"I've brought you something." Darren pulled a thin, dog-eared book out of his pocket and thrust it at Terry.

Not sure how he was supposed to react, Terry took the book. "*Blott and Bitepenn!* Where on Earth did you dig this up?"

Darren grinned. "I kind of took it with me when I left."

Flicking through the pages, Terry shook his head. "This was ancient when I started. We haven't used it for years." He pushed the book back. "Please, keep it. For old times' sake."

"I've done one or two of the tests," Darren said, pulling a couple of sheets of A4 out of another pocket and rubbing them smooth on Terry's desk. "Is this one right?"

Automatically, Terry looked to where Darren was pointing. "Yes, that's right, but…"

"And this one?"

"Nearly, but look, *Blott and Bitepenn* is a book for Year Sevens."

"You used it with us in Year Eleven."

"I don't think…"

"You did." Darren was still smiling but he was insistent. His voice took on the sing-song tone of recollection. "You said we were, '*Acting like kids from a junior school,*' so you'd, '*Give us the work to match.*'"

Terry shifted uncomfortably at this revival of long-buried memories. 5F and the bitter, exhausting struggle between one wet-behind-the-ears teacher and the most evil bunch of little shits God had ever put upon the planet. Or so it had seemed at the time. It had been years since he'd recalled their shockingly poor behaviour. Or his own. "I... don't do that kind of thing anymore."

"Kids these days not as bad, eh?"

"They're pretty much the same, actually. No, it's my classroom management: it's a lot better now. I was in my first year of teaching when I had you, you know? Twenty three and straight out of college."

"Christ! You didn't look that young."

"Thanks."

"But, I don't care." Darren slid back the papers Terry had tried to return. "I couldn't do these exercises then. I've done them now, and I'd like you to have a look at them."

"Darren," Terry said, struggling to remain polite. "I'm sorry, but it's getting late and I'm..."

"Giving up?"

"What?"

"You used to say that a lot. *I'm giving up.*"

"I—. That was years ago. Things are different now. *I'm different now.*"

"But you're still giving up."

"Maybe because you're still acting like a bloody difficult kid." Terry stopped, took a deep breath, and forced an unconvincing laugh. He'd been perilously close to losing his temper. It had been a long day. He was tired. And the reminder of his early failings as a teacher had stung. "Look, I'm sorry. I shouldn't have—"

"You couldn't control us, could you?" Darren grinned again, but the humour of it was gone.

"What? It's not about *control.*"

"All right, you couldn't *manage* us."

"You were sixteen for God's sake, about to leave school."

Even as he snapped at the young man, Terry knew he shouldn't, knew he should stop. But he couldn't. Who did this Darren think he was? "Most of you couldn't even fill in a paperboy's application form properly, but did you want to sit down and actually learn something that would help you when you went out into the 'real world'? Oh no. You were far happier making life a misery for whatever poor sod was trying to teach you!" He stopped, glaring at the other man.

Disconcertingly, Darren was glaring back. "Thick."

"I didn't say that."

"As good as!" And now, with an explosion of rage, Darren surged to his feet and flung "Blott and Bitepenn" across the classroom. "I'm nearly thirty and I still can't get all the answers in a book that's too dumb for little kids!"

Appalled, Terry shoved his chair backwards, ready to run for it if this man went for him.

"Those forms. Paperboy's job? Brickies' job? Signing on? Letters to school? I still can't fill 'em in. Not properly. Not without showing everyone what a thick bastard I am."

Terry forced himself to sound calm, soothing. "I said, you're not…"

"*Slow* then. *Remedial*. Or *special*. With *needs*. Whatever they called it then, that was what this school decided I was, and that was why it put me in classes with thugs like Geoff Young. And teachers like you."

"They were your mates."

Darren's fist smashed into the desk. "They weren't my 'mates'. I hated them. And they hated me."

"But, you said—" Terry frowned in confusion, looking round the classroom, the same room he's begun he'd teaching career in. They'd sat at the back, hadn't they, Geoff and the others? And Darren… He looked down at the desk right in front of his own, the desk Darren was standing behind now. "You sat there."

"And you couldn't see me."

"Of course I saw you."

"Yeah? You never spoke to me, not after you'd called the register. But you'd talk to them wouldn't you, to the 'difficult' ones?"

"I… You don't understand. You have to—"

"You know they used to laugh at you, Geoff and the others? Because you were so easy to wind up. And whenever you lost it, they knew you'd give us one of those 'unsuitable books', and tell us to shut up and get on with it. Geoff and his mates pissed themselves laughing 'cause they could do that stuff with their eyes closed. But I couldn't. And you never helped. *Sit down! Shut up! Get on with it!* That's what you said." Darren looked down at his hand, still bunched into a fist. "I hated you then."

Terry flushed. "I—"

"And you know what made it even worse? I knew that you liked them more than me. Because they were 'lads' weren't they? If Geoff answered a question it'd be, '*Yes Geoff. That's right Geoff. You really are quite bright, aren't you Geoff? If only you'd try a little harder.*' You even put that in his report, didn't you? You knew he tore that up and threw it away on the way home?"

Terry shook his head. "Kids like that respond to the positive. You have to—"

"You were grateful!"

Instinctively, Terry went to deny the accusation. Then

found that he couldn't. "Why did you come back today, Darren?"

"Had to, didn't I? Wanted to see if you'd changed. If you were any better."

Terry swallowed. "I am. Like I said, that was a long time ago."

"And I've got a kid now. A boy."

"Ah. Right." Finally, Terry thought he understood. You could hide illiteracy for years from practically everyone, but not your own kids. "Will you be sending him here?"

"Already do. He started last month. Not having too good a time of it, though. Being bullied. Like I was. I've just been in to see the Head of Year about it before I came to see you."

Terry's eyes narrowed. An uneasy suspicion stirred. "Who does he have for English?"

"You."

In his head, Terry ran through his Year Seven class. "I don't teach a Taylor."

"He uses his mum's name. We're not married. He's a quiet lad, like me when I was here. Not too good at the old reading and writing either, though he's a lot keener than I was. I told him to ask for help but the thing is, he doesn't think the teachers like him. '*They never talk to me, Dad,*' he says. '*I don't think they even know I'm there.*'"

He was a better teacher now. He *was*. But, Terry had to ask. "What's your son's name?"

"He sits here. Right where I am now." Darren looked straight into the eyes of the teacher in front of him. "So. You tell me."

# REMEMBERING FRANK

STEVE BURFORD

Sorry. I must look a right state. I'll be all right in a minute. Pull myself back together. It's just, I've been remembering Frank.

It's not like I've ever forgotten him, of course. You don't forget your big brother. But, well, time goes on doesn't it? And it's right what they say. At first, all you can feel is the sadness, and you don't think that will ever go away. But then it does, and you're left with the good memories to take with you for the rest of your life. Years and years. So strange to think that Frank would be in his eighties now if he was still with us.

It's not as if Jeff looks like him. I went along with it when Carol said, "Look, Mum. He's the spitting image of Uncle Frank." But he wasn't really. He didn't look like him then and he certainly doesn't look like him now, and he's about the same age now as Frank was when he died. Funny. That hadn't struck me before.

He's been a good grandson has Jeff. Cards at Christmas,

visits on my birthday and lovely thank you letters for any presents I sent him, though I think our Carol was behind a lot of those, and they have dried up a bit lately. Well, no-one writes letters any more, do they? I was a bit surprised though when he phoned up out of the blue to say he was going to be dropping by today, and was it all right if he brought a friend, Ceri? "Of course it is," I said, "though Tuesday is my shopping day." I wondered if Ceri might be his girlfriend. I'd never seen any of his girlfriends, so I thought perhaps this one might be a bit special. I thought Ceri was a girl's name.

Less than half an hour after that, Carol rings. We get the usual out of the way and then she says Jeff's going to be calling on me. "I know," I say. She tells me he'll have someone with him, and I say I know that too. "He's a good lad," she says, and I presume she means Jeff. She says her goodbyes and goes, and I remember thinking it was a bit of an odd call.

Of course, when Jeff turned up, I saw straight away that Ceri was a boy. Young man, I should say. They get touchy about that, young fellas, don't they? Tall, skinny lad. Very pale, with blonde hair and glasses. The sort of lad our dad would have called a long drink of water. He seemed nice enough. Bit nervous but I've noticed that with some kids when they meet someone old. It's as if they're scared we might do something odd. Die maybe.

I make them tea and say sorry there isn't any cake or biscuits, but like I said, Tuesday is my shopping day, so at the moment I'm all out of stuff. Jeff laughs and says that's, "No problem," and we all sit and drink our tea and chat, mostly about what he's been up to ("Not much") and what I've been up to ("Even less").

Then he tells me. "Thing is Gran. I'm gay and Ceri is my boyfriend."

"Oh, right." I nod at Ceri, smile and raise my tea cup a little as if I'm toasting him. But inside I'm thinking, *Did I hear him right? Is he joking? What does it mean? Does that mean what it used to mean? What does he want me to say? What does he want me to do?* "Does your mum know?" I say.

"Yeah."

Of course she does. That was why she'd rung me. "Right. Well, I hope you'll be very happy together."

Ceri looked startled. Jeff laughed. "We're not getting married, Gran."

"I was married when I wasn't much older than you." I don't know why I said that either.

"Times change, Gran."

*Yes, they certainly do.* "Well then. I'll go and get my shopping bags, shall I?"

I can't begin to work out how many times I've walked up and down our high street. There's fewer and fewer people there that I know as the years go by, but I still manage to bump into a fair few most days. I hoped I wouldn't see any of them today. We weren't talking about it, but I was still trying to think about what Jeff had told me. Trying to 'process it' – that's what they say nowadays, isn't it?

Sure enough though, I clocked Maisie Davis on the opposite side of the road in the first two minutes. "I'm just popping into here," I said to Jeff and Ceri. They looked surprised, and I couldn't blame them. We were outside a petshop, and heaven only knows what I would have had to buy if I'd gone in. But I was too slow. "Maureen," Maisie called out, and she came trotting across the road. If it hadn't recently been made one way, she'd have been knocked down on the spot. "Hello, love. How you doing then? And who's these two handsome men holding your bags?"

"This is my grandson Jeff, our Carol's boy," I said. "You've heard me talk about him."

"Oh yes. Hello, love." Maisie nodded and smiled at Jeff. Then she looked at Ceri and waited.

"And this is his friend."

There was a bit of a pause. "Well, nice to meet you too," Maisie said. "Anyway, I'd better dash. See you later in the week?"

"You going in then, Gran?" Jeff pointed at the pet shop after Maisie had gone.

I pretended to look at my list. "Actually, we can leave that for the minute, love. On to the bakers."

We walked on, Jeff and Ceri smiling, Jeff pointing out the places he's known since he was a kid. They didn't look annoyed with me. But I was annoyed with me. I was remembering Frank. And Derek.

I'd always assumed Frank and Derek had been at school together. Looking back, that seems unlikely. Softly-spoken, bookish Derek wasn't anything like the other boys from Frank's secondary modern. He wasn't much like Frank either. But for a while, they were inseparable. They'd go walking together, like Jeff and Ceri, side by side.

———

"Hello, Maureen." It was Freda. I've known her since we had our kids at much the same time. I'll often have a coffee with her of a Tuesday.

"Hello, Freda, love. Can't stop. Bit of a rush. See you later in the week?"

"Oh. All right." Freda looked at the lads. "Nice to see you've got a bit of a hand today."

"This is my grandson, Jeff. Our Carol's boy."

"Hello, Jeff." She waited.

"And this is Ceri. He's Jeff's friend."

"Hello, Ceri. Well, see you later, Maur. Bye."

We walked on, and I thought about Derek. That was what he had been: Frank's 'friend'. "Jeff's friend Derek is coming round for tea," Mum would say. "Are you seeing your friend Derek tonight, love?" she'd ask Frank. Dad didn't call him that. Dad didn't talk about him at all, not until that night when Frank told them that he and Derek were going on holiday together. Cornwall, I think it was. Or maybe Devon. I know I'd wanted to go with them but Frank had laughed and said, "Not this time, Maur."

That had been when there'd been the big argument. Dad had been so angry. I'd never seen him that furious. Mum had cried and cried. I'd thought it was because Frank was going on holiday for the first time without us, and Mum and Dad had wanted to go too like I did. I thought perhaps Dad was jealous of Derek. I could tell he didn't like Derek, even though he'd never said it out loud. But that was just the way Dad was. Men were different in those days. You didn't expect them to like everyone.

Frank went on holiday, and I thought that was that. But

soon after he came back, Frank moved out. I cried then, but Frank said it was okay and that I could come and visit him, when I was a little older. But he was killed not longer after. Knocked down in a street much like this one. They didn't let me go to the funeral. They said I was too young. I wonder now if they let Derek go. I hope so. I never saw him again after that.

———

"You don't half know a lot of people, Gran," said Jeff.

"That's the way it is, when you're old."

"That must be nice," said Ceri. "No-one talks to anyone where I was brought up. I'd like to live somewhere where people say hello as you walk down the street."

Frank had been like that. Always a cheery wave and a hello. Used to drive us mad, it did.

We nearly made it back to the car, but then Ralph and Eileen came round the corner. "Hello there, Maureen. Couple of young servants with you today?"

Jeff and Ceri were smiling, waiting for me to say something vague so that we could get on. I nearly did, but I was still thinking of Frank, open, honest Frank, and all the friends he should have had. "This is my grandson, Jeff, our Carol's son." Silly really, but then I took a deep breath. "And this is his boyfriend, Ceri."

I looked at Ralph and I looked at Eileen. I suddenly felt as though I might have done something much bigger than seemed possible with so few words. I felt a bit scared. I felt a bit sad. But I felt right.

Eileen smiled. "Hello," she said to Jeff and Ceri. "Nice to meet you."

"Hello," said Bill and he reached out and shook both boys' hands.

Back home, we unpacked my bags. I put the kettle on and insisted the boys stayed for a 'proper' cup of tea with a piece of cake. There was something I wanted to show them.

"This is Jeff, just after he was born," I said, handing over one of the framed photos I keep on the Welsh dresser.

"Gran!" Jeff protested, though he was grinning.

Ceri had to put his cake and coffee down to take it. "Aw! He's so cute."

I took the picture off him, and handed him the one I really wanted him to see. "And this is his great uncle Frank, my brother. He'd have been about your age when this was taken." Ceri took the picture. I could tell he was puzzled as to why I was showing it to him. "His mother used to say that Jeff looked like him," I said, as if that was an explanation.

Ceri frowned as he studied the picture. "I'm not sure I can see it," he said, obviously trying not to hurt my feelings. "Perhaps a bit about the eyes. Good-looking man though." He looked up at me. "Sorry, I hope you don't mind my saying that."

"Not at all, love." I laughed "And I never thought Jeff looked much like him either."

The boys looked a bit confused, but they both laughed. Well, you've got to humour your batty old relatives, haven't you? They left not long after that. Jeff said they'd both be around again soon to give me another hand with the shopping, but I don't suppose I'll see either of them this side of Christmas.

So, there you go. Funny old day. I'm guessing that, by now Eileen will have told Freda who will tell Maisie all about Ceri. So, I won't have to do that again. Except I want to. I pick up the picture of my lovely, handsome, brave older brother, and I rest one finger on his cheek. I want to tell them about Frank too.

# INTERNAL MONOLOGUE

## STEVEN BURFORD

*I hope he comes over.*

*I hope he doesn't come over.*

*I hope he does.*

*I hope he doesn't.*

*Do it!*

*Don't do it!*

"All right?"

Darren looks up. He has to shield his eyes against the morning winter sun streaming from behind Matt, throwing his face into shadow. "All right."

Matt stands there. It's cold, so he's got his hands in his pockets, but he isn't wearing his blazer of course, and his tie's not done up. "All right if I sit down?" He jerks an elbow at the bench Darren's sitting on. It makes the question casual, like he doesn't give a stuff one way or the other.

"Suppose." *Why're you asking?*

Matt nods and drops himself onto the bench. The two boys sit there. Across the asphalt they can see their mates, and the thousand plus other kids who aren't their mates, kicking balls, scarfing sandwiches, running, jumping, punching, doing all the things you have to do after a long morning of lessons with the prospect of even more to follow. After a couple of minutes of this, Matt finally speaks. "Wow," he says.

*Typical*, thinks Darren. "Yeah, wow," he says. He sits and waits for Matt to set the shape of his new world.

"Did you know you were going to do that?"

*Not the question I was expecting.* "Not really. I knew I was going to do it at some point. I didn't know exactly when though." Darren wrinkles his nose. "I suppose I was just waiting for the right time."

Matt snorts. "And Monday morning, PSHE was your best bet?"

"It was something 'Personal' and 'Social'."

"Not very 'Healthy'."

"Probably not very 'Educational' either. But we were talking about 'relationships'. Seemed like the best time. I couldn't have done it in Home Ec. Or French." Darren thinks for a moment. "Definitely couldn't have done it in French. I don't know the words."

"Je suis gay?" Matt suggests. "J'aime les garçons. Je suis un…"

"Me too." Darren grins.

"Fuck off," Matt says.

*But he's not angry,"* Darren thinks. *At least, I don't think he's angry. He could have been. He could have been furious. He could have come over here to punch me in the face.* Darren's hands are in his pockets too. They're balled into fists. Just in case.

"You could have lied."

"Like the rest of you?" Darren adopts a sing-song, falsetto. 'What am I looking for in a girlfriend, Mr Taylor? Oh, someone I can respect and who'll respect me.'" He mimes vomiting.

"Jayden wasn't going to say that. He was dying to say…"

"I know what Jayden was dying to say. And so did Mr Taylor, which was why he didn't ask him." Darren shakes his head. "I dunno. Maybe if Taylor had said 'partner' I'd have fudged it. But he didn't. He said 'girlfriend'. 'What are you looking for in a girlfriend?' And I'm not." He looks Matt straight in the eye. "Not now, not ever." *Over to you, mate.*

Matt sits, thinking this through. "Fair play to him, though. Taylor took it in his stride."

*And he ducks, dives and avoids the subject.* "They probably train them how to deal with that kind of thing in college."

"Suppose." Across the playground they see Jayden. It looks like he's punching a Year Seven boy. The boy doesn't seem to mind. "Can't imagine old Powell taking it so calmly." The two lads take a moment to picture the crumbly Mr. Powell reacting to someone in his PSHE class outing himself. "Mind you, everyone says Powell's gay himself."

"Yeah, because they don't like him."

"Suppose."

Another minute goes by.

"You have been lying though, haven't you?" Matt doesn't look at Darren while he says this. He keeps his eyes on Jayden, who's moved on to a Year Eight boy now, snatching his basketball and refusing to give it back. "All this time, pretending you're not, y'know…"

*Gay.*

"…when actually, all the time, you were. Not that I blame you," he adds quickly.

*Yes, you do.* "It's not like that. I've not been lying. I've just… not been saying. It's different." Darren looks at Matt, trying to work out what he's thinking. It feels odd looking straight into his friend's face, trying to read it rather than just see it. Time was, less than an hour ago in fact, he would have known what Matt was thinking because, nine times out of ten, it would have been what Darren was thinking anyway. *Does it feel different for you, too?*

"So…"

*Here it comes.*

Matt shifts uncomfortably. It's like he's forgotten how to sit on a bench. "Do you fancy me, then?"

Darren keeps him hanging: he can't help himself. Then, "No," and he laughs.

"Okay."

"Not now, not ever."

"Okay, okay."

*Ten. Nine. Eight. Seven…*

"Why not?"

*Faster than I expected.* "Because. Because you're Matt. You're my best mate." *Aren't you?* "Because, it'd be weird. Like fancying a brother." Again, the temptation is just too strong. "Now, if we were talking about *your* brother…"

Matt's look of horror cracks Darren up. He yanks his hands out of his pockets and waves them in denial. "No, no, no. We are not going there."

"Why not? He's a looker is Kevin. And he's seventeen, so it's not like it'd be illegal." Abruptly, Darren sobers. "Actually,

I suppose it would be, wouldn't it? Me being fifteen. I'd be a criminal." He raises his eyebrows. "Wow."

"Stop pratting about," says Matt, eager to move the conversation away from his family. "Is there anyone that you really do, y'know, fancy?"

Darren puts his pleasure at winding Matt up, and his own newly-discovered legal anxieties, to one side to focus on the question. "No-one actually real, no. Lots of guys off telly and films. That swimmer who's gay. A couple of football players."

"Yeah?" At the mention of football, Matt brightens. "Who?" Then he recollects himself. "Never mind."

"It's cool. They're from City."

Matt frowns. He's not sure if Darren's still taking the piss, or even if it's a good thing that Darren's staying loyal to their team. He presses on. "But, if you haven't got..."

*You can't say it, can you?"*

"I mean, if there isn't anyone you..., you know, then... how do you know?"

"You haven't got a girlfriend."

"Yes I have!"

Darren folds his arms. "A quick fumble in the queue at Maccy D's does not make Mia your girlfriend. And that's what she said."

Matt goes to retort, and for a second, Darren wishes he would, that they could let this conversation descend into familiar, comfortable banter. *But we can't, can we? Not until we've sorted this. If we can.*

"I just know," says Matt.

Darren nods. "Yeah. Me too." *Get it?*

From the buildings across the yard come three piercing electronic notes: the summons back to lessons.

*Now or never.* Darren turns on the bench to face Matt. He's hunched over, staring at the gum-pocked tarmac as if it's a maths problem he's trying to work out. "We still mates, then?" He's pleased that his voice sounds level because his heart feels like it's in his throat and is going to burst.

Matt looks up. "Suppose," he says. He sounds surprised, perhaps by the question, perhaps by his answer. "I mean, it doesn't really matter these days, does it?"

*Not if you're straight. But will you stay my mate when they start asking you why you're hanging around with me? Will you stick up for me when they make jokes about 'queers' and 'paedos', even if I'm not there, or will you pretend you haven't heard? Or will you join in? And when I do get a boyfriend…?*

Suddenly, Darren wants to touch Matt, to hold or hug him. The strength of it almost takes his breath away. And it's not because he fancies him but because he knows that Matt does mean what he's saying, that he will try his hardest. And right now, Darren loves him for that. "No. It doesn't really matter," he says.

Matt stands. "I'm gonna go and get a quick baguette before Music. Coming?"

"In a minute."

Darren remains sitting on the bench, watching his mate walk away from him and into the main school building. Step by step, he gets further away. *Will we ever be that close again?* Darren wonders.

He also wonders when he started talking to himself so much.

Across the yard, two Year Sevens chase each other round and round in circles, shrieking and laughing, making the most of the last few seconds of break. Darren remembers when he and Matt had been like that. It could have been yesterday. It was yesterday. He hadn't used to talk to himself then. He hadn't needed to. He'd had Matt. The young lads start thumping each other. It looks like it's making them happy. *Not much talking to themselves going on in those heads.*

Darren stands, squares his shoulders, and begins the walk back into school. *Time, literally, to face the music.* He takes one last look at the giggling Year Sevens. *Wankers!*

# THE NIGHTINGALE

ANIL CLASSEN

Suad was so caught up in her singing that she failed to hear the sound of his key in the door. His key ring was so full that the chorus of metal chimes would normally have her ears pricked up. It was the perfect alarm system. The hand on her shoulder was so unexpected that she almost screamed. She had not heard his footsteps because he had taken his shoes off, as was the habit since they moved to Hamburg. The city was so different from Kabul that it may as well have been on another planet. Suad felt the air sucked out of her, the last sung note still hanging in the air for a moment before it vanished like a startled fairy.

'How long have you been singing?'

The question sounded simple. It demanded a simple answer. Suad took in his enlarged eyes that were framed by a pair of thick black spectacles. She saw the anger vibrate in time with the throbbing vein on his forehead.

'Suad, I asked you a question. How long have you been…*singing*?'

This second question was accompanied by his firm hands applying more pressure to her shoulder. She tried to twist herself free but it was pointless. She could already feel the shiver of pain coursing down her left arm all the way to her hand that was still holding the green and white striped sweater she had been folding before he appeared like a bad-tempered genie.

'Not long.'

Her answer was soft, lost in the small bedroom.

He shook her shoulders before he shouted, 'How long?'

They were so engrossed in each other that neither of them heard the approaching footsteps before Suad felt her body being pulled from her father's strong grip.

'Are you crazy?'

It was her mother, her brown eyes wild with confusion as she wrapped Suad in her arms.

'I was only…' he tried to say before his eyes fell to the ground. This lasted only a moment before he raised his head, his eyes different, as if he had suddenly remembered something.

'She cannot sing in the apartment. The neighbours… the Ahmeds, they… they will hear her.'

'And? So what if they do? What were you thinking?' she hissed. 'You scared her!'

There was a long pause before he walked away. A few seconds later her mother stood up and left the room, foolishly forgetting to close the door, allowing her daughter access to the argument that was already starting in the kitchen. Suad pressed her face between the cracked wooden doorway and the door handle that felt cold against her cheek.

'I will not have her singing… she is no longer a child.'

'She's just turned eight… of course she's a child!'

Suad could see the side of her jeans, the pair that sat snugly on her hips, the pair they had bought together in a store that offered so many styles that it overwhelmed both of them. They had never experienced such a myriad of choice before, nor the amount of bare skin around them.

'We've spoken about this.'

'No, *you* spoke about this… this madness.' Her voice dropped a notch as she continued, 'I was silly to think it was a mood, Ismael…'

Now her voice softened as she said his name. Suad recognised the sugared tone. This tactic had been used on her to calm her moods or to lift her spirits.

'Leila, I will not have the neighbours gossiping about our daughter… or our lack of morals,' he said, regrouping. 'She is over eight years now. She is not allowed to sing in this home… or anywhere else anymore.'

Suad closed her eyes. She felt the beginnings of shame. It followed the rumbling in her tummy. She knew that she should have been more careful. Her father had warned her. But she could not stop herself from singing, though. The song had ripped its way through her when she discovered the rare intimacy of being alone in the apartment. Her mother had shushed her last week as she started humming her favourite Disney song, the one every girl in her class was singing, the one her teacher had told them to please stop singing because it was unbearable.

'This is craziness.'

'You call our religion crazy?'

Her father's slow tone sounded scary all of a sudden. 'You think that what we believe in… is crazy?'

'Tell me why we moved here, Ismael... tell me why I gave up everything... *everything* I knew to follow you here, to this country where everyone looks at me like I am an alien because I choose to wear a scarf over my head. Tell me.'

'You know why we moved.'

'I want to hear it from you. Even if it is the fiftieth time, Ismael.'

There was a light groan before he answered, 'Because there was no future for us in Afghanistan.'

'And now our future here is meant to be one of restriction? You expect me to believe that because some man in the mosque is preaching that our daughter should no longer sing, that it is okay? What's next? Will you force me to wear hijab? Will you lock me up in this apartment just to avoid other men looking at me?'

'For goodness' sake, lower your voice. You are bordering on blasphemy... the Ahmeds...'

Suad knew the mistake even as he was still speaking. Her mother did not enjoy being interrupted, nor did she enjoy being told to be silent.

'I don't care about our nosy neighbours, Ismael! They can listen all they want. You promised me that things would be different here. We ran away from all that...'

'All that what?'

'You know what,' she said in a lower voice, forcing Suad to squeeze her head further into the doorway so she could hear better.

'This was meant to be a new start. You have been different since you found your new friends. When you grew your beard, I thought you looked even more handsome. Now I know it was only so you can fit in here. Your friends are no different from those you ran from.'

'And what's that supposed to mean?'

'Your friends back home turned on you because of your work… they all turned their backs on your friendship. To them you were a traitor because you translated German texts. Suddenly you were going against your religion just because you were trying to put food on the table for your family.'

Suad remembered the angry faces of the men that day. She could still feel her mother grabbing at her arm as she foolishly unlatched the key chain, allowing them space to barge in and drag her father away.

'It was more complicated than that. These are good people here, Leila. If you took the time to get to know them… you would…'

'I have taken the time!' she suddenly yelled. 'I met their wives. I went to their homes as you asked me to. Do you know what their daughters said to Suad?'

'What?'

'That her scarf is too colourful. She should wear black. And the worst of it was,' she said forcefully before her voice faltered. 'The worst is that… all the mothers nodded. One of them actually turned to Suad and told her that the last thing she surely wanted was the boys noticing her.'

'Were they wrong?'

'Can you even hear yourself? We ran from these people!' she yelled again. 'These people who now want you to put a muzzle on your daughter like she's some sort of dog that does not know better.'

'You are blowing this out of proportion.'

'Am I? It seems you and I are on two byways, Ismael, and

sooner or later one of us is going to grow tired of travelling alone.'

The sound of a chair being pushed backwards echoed down the hallway before her mother called, 'Suad! We're going out.'

'Where are you going?'

The open shock laced its way through her father's thin voice.

'Are you now monitoring me as well? Is that who you want to be? One of *those* men… those men you rolled your eyes at before? I am taking my daughter for a walk… if that is okay with you?'

Half an hour later Suad found herself in front of a middle eastern restaurant. She turned her face to smile at her mother whose eyes were masked by angry clouds that managed the impossible task of making her even prettier.

'Why are we here? It isn't my birthday.'

'We don't need a birthday to spoil ourselves.'

Her mother's reply was followed by a sly wink. The clouds dissipated slightly.

'Could we have two portions of sheer pira as a takeaway?' Suad's mother asked politely in Arabic.

The tall woman next to the cash register wore a striking red and white dotted scarf. She nodded before opening a large glass cabinet door that revealed several stands with various desserts on large metal trays. Suad could already taste the earthy ground cardamom on her tongue. When she saw the diamond-shaped pieces of the traditional dessert her grandmother had always prepared for her on special occasions, she closed her eyes, thinking of the thick creaminess mixed with too much syrup and chopped nuts.

As her mother opened her bag to pay, Suad heard someone singing. For a short second, she thought it was the radio, but then the sound intensified. She looked up, into the exasperated eyes of the woman behind the counter.

'That Miriam, she's my pride and joy, but she is like a bird that won't stop chirping.'

Suad felt her mother's eyeing her. She lowered her head before she looked back up into the curious eyes behind the counter.

'She's allowed to sing?' Suad asked.

The question stood uncomfortably in the room until her mother's hand touched her shoulder. Suad's eyes remained glued to the woman who looked at her mother quickly before she focused on Suad again. The understanding passing between the two women was something Suad could not grasp. The three of them stood in silence until the singing in the background grew louder, reminding Suad why she had asked the question.

'Here we sing all we like. No one,' the woman finally said as her face broke into a large smile, 'no one has the right to silence us, habib.'

When they were outside, Suad waited until they had found a bench to sit on before she asked, 'Did I do something wrong?'

Her mother dipped into the white plastic packet on her lap and fished out two plastic dishes holding their treats.

'No, darling.'

'But… I said something wrong in the restaurant, didn't I? And… and you and Daddy… you were fighting because of me.'

'Your father and I… we are still getting used to Hamburg,

Suad. It was no different for you. Remember how scared you were of going to school here?'

Suad nodded before she bit into the solid dessert that almost crumbled between her small fingers. The wave of sugar was almost overwhelming.

'And now you have friends. You enjoy going to school. It just takes time.'

'Can I still sing?'

There was a slight hesitation from her mother. Suad saw the way her smooth forehead rippled into fine lines before she asked, 'Does your singing hurt anyone?'

'Well... no.'

'Then you carry on singing, Suad. You have such a lovely voice. It would be a shame not to use it, don't you think?'

'Do you want me to sing?'

'What, here?' her mother asked before her lips puckered teasingly, matching her cheeky brown eyes.

'If you like,' Suad said shyly.

'Well, by all means... don't let me stop you.'

Suad's legs dangled freely above the ground before she started singing. A jogger ran by, turning her blonde head slowly to the sound of the pretty voice that rose up from the dark grey park bench. In that moment, the song Suad had heard in the restaurant left her lips, the Arabic making her mother close her eyes in silent pleasure.

# WHO WILL SING AT DAVY MCGARRY'S FUNERAL?

PETER COLLINS

*'…How great Thou art, how great Thou art.'*

The strong, clear baritone had barely finished before the congregation burst into a spontaneous round of applause. Davy McGarry walked solemnly from the lectern to the edge of the altar, bowed to the priest and made the sign of the cross, then returned to his seat. He was delighted that the mourners had liked his singing, but he kept his expression sombre. After all, this was Paddy Ryan's funeral mass. Later on at the Irish Centre, he could accept their praise and compliments, but now was the time to show respect.

Father O'Hara, never one to hang about, hurried through the rest of the mass and was soon giving the mourners a farewell message.

'Just to let you know that Paddy's family have asked that only relatives and very close friends come to the graveyard, please. But everybody else is more than welcome to come down the Irish Centre to see Paddy off in style.'

Whilst the undertaker stepped forward to organise the

pallbearers to carry the coffin (there was never a shortage of nephews and cousins for such a task at an Irish Catholic funeral) Davy wondered whether he would count as a very close friend and if he should go to the graveyard. He probably should, he decided; he'd known Paddy for forty years and Mary had asked him to sing at the funeral for heaven's sake. But he wouldn't barge in. He'd stand respectfully by the hearse and wait for Mickie or Mary to invite him as they were sure to do.

The mourners slowly filed out behind the coffin and Davy joined the queue, shuffling solemnly along. As he neared the church door, he felt a tap on his shoulder. He turned to see the diminutive figure of Maggie Walsh, without whose say-so, nothing got done in the church.

'Will you be a lamb, Davy, and help me with the hymn books?'

Davy glanced out of the door. He didn't drive so he'd need a lift to the cemetery. But there was still a large crowd of people milling about. It'd be a while yet before the hearse set off.

'Sure, Maggie. No problem.'

He went with Maggie to gather up the hymnals. They lay scattered forlornly around the church like debris after a music festival. Then Maggie caught sight of Father O'Hara and buttonholed him about the children's liturgy leaving Davy to collect the books on his own. There were more than he had thought and when he finally got outside, the hearse had gone. Dark clouds had gathered ominously overhead and the smell of rain was in the air. Davy looked around hopefully for a lift but the rest of the mourners had already headed off to the

Irish Centre. Turning his collar up against the weather, he thrust his hands in his pockets and began to walk.

Walking wasn't a problem for Davy McGarry. He was seventy-six years old but he was still fit. He'd spent his early life on the family farm in County Kerry and then forty years in the building trade here in England. He wasn't a tall man, but he was broad and still well-muscled even in his retirement. His once sandy hair was now grey and his open face was weathered from a lifetime working outdoors. He'd first met Paddy when he'd come over from Ireland and started working for Paddy's brother, Mickie. Davy had a fine voice in those days. He'd lost count of the weddings and funerals he'd been asked to sing at. He'd become a fixture in the Irish community in the town; part of everybody's extended family. Davy had never married. He considered his circle of friends at the Irish Centre to be his family. It was important to Davy to be part of that circle; perhaps more important than anybody knew. Singing was his anchor. His voice wasn't as strong now as it once was. That was only to be expected. But he'd learned a lot over the years and his timing and phrasing was better than it ever was. He still had a few more years left in him.

It was a fair walk to the Irish Centre and the rain had come in earnest. He could see from the cars parked outside that the family had made it back from the cemetery. A broad-shouldered man with a pronounced beer belly wearing a faded green and red Mayo football jersey was sitting by the door reading a dog-eared detective novel, a half-drunk pint of lager on the table in front of him. He nodded a greeting and watched without offering to help as Davy struggled to take off his wet coat.

'Afternoon, Danny,' said Davy hanging his coat in the cloakroom.

Danny Malone, long time doorman and general factotum at the Irish Centre frowned gravely.

'Busy in there, Davy lad,' he said. 'I'd get a few in now if I were you. Save time.'

Davy nodded and headed into the bar. The place was heaving. A few people patted him on the back and congratulated him on his singing as he jostled his way through the crowd. At the bar he bumped into Mickie Ryan.

'Ah, here's the man of the hour. It'd be a poor funeral without you singing, Davy. Will ye have a drink with me?'

Mickie Ryan was a giant of a man and he'd used his intimidating presence to good effect in getting building contracts over the years.

'I'll have a pint, please, Mickie,' said Davy, quietly pleased at Mickie's obvious show of closeness.

'Grand. Tell you what. I have a bit of business to attend to. Could you get them in for us?' Mickie passed a ten pound note across to Davy and levered himself away from the crush.

Davy queued for the two pints. His lack of height and less commanding presence meant he was easily overlooked in the crowd and it was a while before he got served. Eventually he made his way into the main room with the two pints.

'Davy, over here,' a voice shouted over the noise.

He turned towards the voice. Danny Malone was struggling to bring some trestle tables into the room.

'There must be close on two hundred people here. The girls are busy getting more food ready and they didn't put out enough tables. Can you help me with these?'

'I'm just taking this to Mickie,' Davy replied holding up

the pint.

'He's in the back room with Mary. This'll only take a minute.'

Davy looked around helplessly for a moment but he could see Danny was struggling. He put the pints on one side and began to help Danny bring out more tables and chairs.

'It shows what a popular man Paddy was,' said Davy indicating the throng of people as they carried out the last table.

Danny just snorted. 'It shows what some shameless feckers will do for free sausage rolls and chicken wings.'

They set up the tables and as Danny headed back to his place on the door Davy retrieved his pints and headed to the small office at the back of the Centre. Inside he found Mickie with his son, Tommy and Paddy's wife, Mary all sitting round a table with a large stack of white envelopes in front of them.

'Ah, cheers there, Davy lad,' said Mickie, reaching for the proffered pint and downing half of it one large gulp.

'Tommy, Mary,' Davy nodded his respects.

'Ah that was beautiful singing, there, Davy,' acknowledged Mary with a sad smile. She was a slender woman and the black dress she wore seemed two sizes too large for her. 'Himself would have been pleased to hear it.'

'Anything for Paddy, Mary, you know that. He was like family to me.'

Davy looked down at the table and saw a pile of small cards, no larger than playing cards, each with a photo of Paddy on the front.

'Are they the memorial cards, Mary? Jeez, you're quick off the mark and no mistake.'

'It was Paddy's wish, Davy. He wanted me to get the cards ready for family and close friends as soon as we could.'

Mary continued to place a card inside each envelope as she spoke. Mickie downed the rest of his pint and stood up.

'Right then. Well I'll leave you to it. I'd best get out and socialise.'

Tommy spoke up. He was large and ruddy faced like his father. 'Dad, before you go.' He raised his hand and rubbed his thumb and fingers together in the universal sign for money. 'We'll need something to tip the staff.'

Mickie reached for his pocket.

'How much?'

'Well, there's Danny Malone, the three lads on the bar, and there's at least four of the girls doing the food. Best make it two hundred. We can't be mean with the hired help.'

Mickie stared at Davy in mock despair. 'Jeez, the little fecker'll bleed me dry.' But he was already peeling the notes from a large wad of twenties.

Davy followed Mickie back to the bar. The party was in full swing now. Beers were being drunk and a lot people had begun to reminisce about the old days. A few people slapped him on the back and congratulated him on his singing. One of Paddy's old workmates (Declan, or was it Conor?) bought him another pint. The night seemed to go by in a blur. A number of people asked him to sing something. He was flattered, but out of respect for Paddy he decided not to.

At the end of the evening he saw Tommy tip the bar staff and caterers, and then watched with interest as Mary and Mickie discretely sought out members of the inner circle of Paddy's friends and family and passed each of them a white envelope. Tommy caught his eye and wandered over.

'Thanks again, Davy. This is for you.' He handed over a small white envelope.

Davy nodded his thanks and put the envelope in his pocket. He was filled with a quiet pride at receiving the memorial card. He didn't really know why that should be; he'd known Paddy a long time and they'd become close over the years. It was only natural that he should be included, but it gave him a warm feeling inside. Davy considered opening the envelope there to have a proper look at the memorial card, but he thought that might be a bit insensitive to the people who hadn't received one. He decided it could wait until he got home.

He said his goodbyes and set off on the short walk home. It was still raining and he was glad to reach the shelter of his flat. He took off his coat, turned on the small electric fire and poured himself a generous measure of Jameson's. He raised the glass in a toast.

'Here's to you, Paddy. May God rest you.'

He sipped the whiskey appreciatively and settled into his chair. Davy picked up the white envelope and opened it slowly. As he did so, the single piece of paper it contained slipped from his fingers and dropped to the floor. He looked at it for a while without attempting to pick it up. He took another sip of his whiskey and sat back in his chair, his eyes glassy and unfocussed as he stared unseeingly at the flickering gas flame for a long while. He dug his fingers into the arms of the chair as if to check it was real. The chair seemed solid enough, but despite that Davy could feel his whole world crumbling about him. Who would have thought that a single piece of paper could be so devastating? He bent down to pick it up. Not the memorial card given to close friends and family but a crisp twenty pound note paid out to the hired help.

# VULTURES WITH MACHINE GUNS

## MARK DEMEZA

My mobile phone beeped plaintively. Looking down, I saw the flashing image of an empty battery and an exclamation mark. Then, the screen went blank. I pressed the restart button several times, but there was no response. Now I was alone, quite alone.

I had been outside Kabul airport for three days now. It had been pandemonium. The area was seething with people bustling in every direction, desperately looking; looking for family, for friends, for colleagues, for contacts who might help them beat the queues. Looking for a way out.

It was as if a new village had formed where we stood. Fruit sellers had set up with freshly cut, crimson-pipped pomegranates glistening on rickety mobile stalls. The smell of grilled meat drifted in the air, tainted with the stench of latrines that had been set up in disused gullies and ditches. Tattered sheets had been draped across the women's facilities to protect their modesty. Hawkers darted about the crowds, but I never saw anybody have time to stop and buy.

The Taliban peered down on us like attendant vultures. Vultures with machine guns. They used any way to raise themselves above the height of the crowds around them. They stood on car roofs, on oil barrels, on low, flat roofed buildings. They were everywhere. On their own, or in small groups, sinisterly whispering into each other's ears.

Some wore traditional, white peraahan tunbaan clothing. Some wore uniforms stolen from Afghan army soldiers, the spoils of war. Some even wore US military uniforms, perhaps from a little last-minute bartering with the enemy. But every single one had a gun in his hands, muzzle pointing directly at the masses before them.

We were terrified of staying. And terrified of leaving.

After hours of persuading, cajoling, and begging, I found myself in the final queue. Like a human funnel, we were being guided into a gap of around a metre between two forty-foot steel containers. In the searing sunlight, the containers themselves had risen to a baking temperature, scalding to the touch, like being wedged between two electric heaters. But I shuffled on. We all did. I could not go backwards; I could only go forwards with the snail-paced momentum of the queue.

In single file, nobody spoke. All that could be heard was the scratching of feet on yellowed grit, and the incessant hubbub of people beyond our steel cage, buzzing like an increasingly enraged swarm of hornets.

I was desperate to relieve myself. I did not want to humiliate myself, and yet I could not lose my place in the queue. I feared the reprobation of the people in front of and behind me. In the end I could wait no longer. I loosened the azaar-band of my harem trousers and sighed as the pressure eased.

Nervously looking from side to side, I could see that no one was looking or watching or bothering.

"It's okay." A voice spoke softly behind me.

I turned to see a short man, perhaps forty years old and with bright blue eyes that flitted around, nervously taking in the Taliban soldier who loomed above us on the roof of the container. He was wearing a peraahan tunbaan suit, plain blue, edged with striking and unusual golden stitching.

"The Afghan people are known for their civility, culture and hospitality," he continued. "That's all gone now, my friend. It's coming to an end yet again. Perhaps, it'll return once more in the future. Nobody cares about where we piss anymore. It's the least of our worries."

There are many languages and dialects in Afghanistan, but I recognized his Pashto dialect immediately. There are many languages and dialects in Afghanistan, and Pashto is the language of the Taliban.

I immediately looked at the Taliban soldier above us, frightened that he might interpret our talking as suspicious. Fortunately, he was shouting into his walkie talkie and waving his AK-47 at somebody else.

At the far end of the containers, the gap was secured by two British soldiers. One was standing guard, in his mid-twenties, tall and athletic, with pale skin and fair hair. The other was sitting at a small table, of smaller stature and darker hair, and responsible for scrutinising the paperwork that could save my life. I hoped upon hope that I would recognize them, and they me. But their faces were as blank as the desert sands.

As an interpreter, I had stood amongst British soldiers in

Helmand province, in remote villages where the darkness is as black as ink and as silent as a graveyard. I recognized the L11 sniper rifle that the soldier was carrying. I wondered how and why he had come to be using this long-range weapon amongst a closely packed throng like this.

The rifle was slung over his shoulder. That tells a story. In civilian situations, the British bear the rifle over the shoulder and across the back. The weapon is there, but not intended as a first response. The Taliban always stands with finger on trigger, the weapon ready for immediate use. An angry Taliban fighter will have you dead in the blink of an eye. I have seen it many times. Shoot first, no questions, no answers.

My Special Immigrant visa and letter of recommendation were stuffed tightly into my trouser pocket. Folded and covered in dirty marks as if worthless, they were literally life or death documents. If found by the Taliban, and revealing my affiliation with their enemies, it would lead to my summary execution. Down a shadowy alleyway or in a public park, whichever suited them best. Otherwise, these flimsy pieces of paper could give me a meaningful life in another country.

"My name's Adnan." The stranger continued, "It's okay, the Taliban cannot hear us from up there. And between these metal containers, it's far too cramped, and too close to the British Army for them to become engaged." He smiled nervously.

"We can never be too sure. Never," I replied quietly, barely moving my lips.

He must have sensed my reticence.

"Don't worry. I am only a humble schoolteacher. Unfortunately, an English teacher, and nowadays that puts me in the same danger as yourself, no doubt, my friend," he said. He dipped his head reverentially as he spoke.

I made as if to give my name but held back. Who was this guy, with his fancy golden stitching? That's a sign of money, surely? What if he were a Taliban spy? I was too close to freedom to take any risks. At any moment, Taliban could be in this gap, dragging me away. Nothing was too cramped for them. The British could and would do nothing to intervene.

In such a state of fear, it seemed to take hours for the paperwork to be processed. By midday, when the sun was at its highest, I had only moved a little more than half the length of the containers. I tried to stay positive, telling myself that with every step there was more behind me and less in front.

The heat was blistering. Even by Afghan standards.

When we finally neared the end of the containers, I had a glimpse of our next destination. A single story, grey brick building standing several metres beyond, with a door facing us bearing a sign saying, "WARNING. Airside authorisation required beyond this point".

There were only two people between me and the British soldiers. A man and a woman whose voices I had not heard and faces I had not seen. Both dressed in black, to me they looked like featureless shadows. I noticed how their index fingers gently coiled and uncoiled around each other.

I glanced left and right. And upwards. The Taliban had disappeared. I stood on my tiptoes to see a little further, but there were no Taliban. My belly tightened. There was a breeze block lying on the ground. I stood on that too, and from there I could see that there were no Taliban on either container roof.

Strange, I thought.

And then the world caved in.

The noise of the bomb was so loud I thought it had knocked me to the ground on its own. It streamed into my ear drums and seemed to shake my head from the inside, like a cat tossing a mouse in its jaws.

There was dirt and debris everywhere. I gasped a desperate breath of air, and hot dust coursed through my lungs, like fire spreading through a coal mine.

I could barely hear, but as moments passed sounds started to drift through. There was frantic screaming and shouting. One scream was so high and heartrending, it had to be a mother grieving a child, I thought.

"Harry, are you okay?"

I turned my head to the side and saw one of the soldiers on his haunches, shaking his companion.

"Should be," came the reply, "just a bit shaken, Robbie. The containers must have shielded us from the full force of the explosion."

They both stood up, briefly dusted themselves down and looked around. Harry now did have his rifle out, butt nestled against his shoulder, panning from side to side like a periscope.

"This is our flight, Robbie," Harry shouted.

Their gaze met. There was silence as each waited for the other to speak.

"But…" was the only word Robbie could muster.

"This is our flight, Robbie," Harry repeated firmly, before continuing, "there's nothing more we can do here. It's the last flight."

"But we still have five civilian spaces to fill! It's the last flight for them, too!" Robbie replied.

Harry considered for a moment

"Okay, just bring the next five, sod the paperwork for now," Harry urged, glancing at me and the two men directly in front. "Make it snappy!"

I turned around to look behind. The area was still swimming in a sea of dirt. One of the containers had been shunted by the blast, making the gap even narrower.

In a daze, I stood up.

There had been a concrete lamp post between us and the building. The force of the blast had cracked the post, and with a quirk of fate it had toppled into the gap between the two containers. I could see it at my feet, stretching into the distance and disappearing into the fog. It must have fallen just behind me.

"Adnan?" I asked, peering forward.

There was no movement, no sound. I took a step forward.

"Not that way! Not that way! This way!" Robbie was shouting at me. Covered in dust, his face was ghost-like.

I sensed movement from within the gap, silhouettes appeared, making their way forward.

"The next five only!" Robbie ordered.

I made another tentative step forward and deciphered the shape of a man, pinned underneath the post. And a dark coloured garment. My heart stopped when I noticed an intricate stitched hem. Even within this hellish sandstorm, the golden stitching seemed to glow.

I sensed another person moving towards me and heard the barking orders of the British soldiers.

I turned and briskly made my way to the door which was being held open by Robbie. When I had crossed the threshold, I watched as he quickly pulled the door to and firmly slid the bolt into its keep with a resounding thud.

And I followed the others into the airport building.

# THE BLACK KEYS

MARY ELLEN FOX

There is a saying in Azerbaijan: You see the road as you go. I wonder if she had been able to see what lay before her whether she would have chosen a different path? It is hard to say, and I guess I will never know now. I don't like her much and yet there is something about her. Possibly her head is so high in the clouds she does not fear.

This cell smells of shit and damp straw and something metallic. There is a little window set high up in the wall with the bars on the inside. On the floor lies a straw-filled mattress and next to this a plain wooden pail which serves as her nuisance bucket.

'You remember our bargain?' I ask.

'Yes. I remember.'

'I will tell you about my trips to Baku.'

'And I will play the piano for you.'

'I went down to the banks of the Caspian last night.'

'How near?'

'Oh near. By the Maiden Tower.

'And what was the water like?'

'Rough. Oily. Black as tar.'

'Did you sit?'

'Yes, By the Shirvanshah Palace… I drank two armudus of tea.'

'Ooh,' she sighs, as if I have presented her with a diamond choker.

'With jam?'

'Of course.'

'What kind?'

'Quince.'

She closes her eyes then and I know what she is thinking. She is imagining the ripe quinces hanging in her orchard back in Gabala.

I spit a flake of tobacco out onto the dirt floor and take two puffs of the pipe.

Through the window comes the droning sound of the muezzin calling the Islamists to prayer. The fools.

'I must pray first.' She says.

And she unrolls her mat. A tiny thing which she must have brought with her. Along with the dress and the boots and the white stockings like some mountain maid on her way to the milking barn. I suck the tobacco through my teeth. Not much use for dresses and stockings where you're going, madam.

So, she kneels hands above her head and kisses the mat and then stands up, prays some more and kneels again rubbing her face all the while.

'Enough', I cry, and she is silent then. For she knows what that means. She stands and rolls up the mat and places it under the desk.

'You are so talented Gayibova. It's such a shame.'

I quickly regret this last sentence as her fists smash down upon the desk. At the noise, someone cries out from another cell.

'My name is Khadija. Can you say that, you stupid woman? Khadija.'

'I know. Like the Prophet's wife. I know… Khadija.' I so want to hear her play that for this night only I am prepared to humour her. 'Shall we go?'

She continues to sit there, bolt upright, with her fists clenched tight, still resting on the desk lid for a long time, a few minutes perhaps. And then she pulls herself up to her full six feet in height, even taller in the stupid block heels, strides to the door and stands there in silence waiting for me to unlock it.

She walks ahead of me down the corridor back as straight as an iron girder. I follow on, dragging my bad leg behind me. She occasionally looks to the right and gives a half-hearted wave. She knows some of the women in the other cells. The familiar thump scrape of my boots and cane on the concrete alert the women to my presence and they scurry back from the bars into the shadows, like cockroaches doused in oil. A spineless coven. Their finery now in ruins: skirts crusted with shit and mud from the floor, hair straggled and left to silver. Faces spectre-white from lack of sunshine. Sometimes, to upset them, I bang the knob of my cane on the bars.

I can tell they do not like her though. The women. A couple of them wave but most do not look up. I think they believe her too haughty, too above her station. With the stupid dress and the boots and the white stockings. Who does she think she is any way? They never express it to me, but I can tell. Oh, they hate me, but I think they dislike her almost as much. Perhaps they do not want to be tainted by her treachery. Most of them will be let out in a few months, once their husbands have been executed. Or perhaps they feel there is no point in greeting a condemned woman. It is hard to tell. The corridor is almost thirty metres in length. Apart from the occasional clamour of buckets against bars and the soft crying and keening of a few of the older women, the cells are mostly quiet. Gilded in the sunset, her fair plait shines like a crown.

I keep the piano in my office at the end of the corridor. It was my father's and was handed down from his father before him. Rumour has it that it was removed from a bar during the Crimean war and carried to our family home in St Petersburg by four deserting soldiers. I had eight men transport it from St. Petersburg to here. My father played it from childhood. At the thought of him my hand flutters over the locket wherein lies his picture. It is a grainy photo of the back of his head. He wears the cap of the soviet army, and he is playing Kalinka. Many think it strange that I should only have a photo of the back of my father's head, and stranger still that I have a picture of St Piotr in the other half. But old habits are hard to break.

The door falls open with a satisfying click. She rushes to the stool and begins playing something I have not heard before. Unmistakably a Turkic tune. Swaying and lilting to it whilst her thick fair plait, reaching almost to her waist, slides around her back like a coil of oiled rope.

'Not that.' I cry out.

She probably does not hear me for she carries on regardless. So engrossed is she in the melody.

'You know the man of steel was kept here?' I know that will grab her attention.

'What? Stalin? Here?' The blue eyes widen.

'Yes, in block 12. Cell 3.'

'When?' She shrinks back as though the keys have burned her fingertips.'

'Oh, way before your time.'

'Why?'

'He was protecting miners' rights.'

'Hah,' she snorted, 'that evil Georgian dwarf couldn't protect his own mother's goat.'

'Well, you may be twice his height but you're the one locked up now. Just remember that.'

'What shall I play?' she asks wearily as though resigned to the fact that she must keep her side of the bargain.

'Kalinka'. I reply. I am not totally sure, but I think I detect the hint of a smirk playing on her lips.

'You want a Russian folk tune?' she asks.

I say nothing to this and simply watch her stretch her fingers over the octaves just like Papa used to.

'There are two keys missing' she says.

'What?'

'Two white keys. Look. Here and here.'

'Oh yes.' I do not mention the reason for their absence. Do not mention that the keys were broken when I pulled down the lid on the hands of the last person to play in this room. The two white keys were crushed along with the two white fingers.

'Play the black keys only then.' I pull on the stem on my pipe. She appears to ignore me and starts to play in the key of D minor. There seems to be a slight tremble around her mouth as I bring down the brass end of my cane onto one end of the keyboard.

'Remember why you are in here.'

'I do not know why.'

'You are a traitor and a spy.'

'No. My only crime is to compose Mughrab.'

'What those shit Azeri folk songs?' She says nothing. 'You only play Russian songs now. Anything else is anti-Soviet.'

'How?'

'They are backward. Full of superstitious nonsense.'

'No!', she wails, 'No. No. No. You are wrong.'

I do not correct her. For I know there will be no more Azeri folk songs. Not tomorrow nor any other day. Tomorrow the keys will be silenced.

'So, play Kalinka now. With the black keys only. Please.' She looks me full in the face then. The eyes flash blue like the tiny flames at the base of Fire Mountain and the corners of her mouth have turned up again, in that smirk I have come to know so well.  But, nevertheless, she plays the tune with the fluency and passion that she accords all her performances and when it is over, I nod to her to indicate my satisfaction.

There is a light rap on the door. Khadija Gayibova stiffens.

'I have a surprise for you.' I open the door and in runs the daughter. They are bound together by the door with love and smothering kisses, and I remove myself as I feel a lurch in my stomach of disgust and not a little envy at the same time. How pathetic it is to be so jealous of a condemned woman I think to myself as I hobble to the sofa in the alcove at the far end of the room. From here I can just about catch what they are saying:

'Oh mama. You look well. It is so good to see you.'

'Oh, my sweet. Your cheeks are red. Have you been running?'

'Yes. I ran all the way from school. Miss Aleyeva let me out early.'

'That was kind of her.'

'Well, yes. But she gave me the ruler this morning. Look here at my hands.'

'Oh no. Why?'

'I kicked Nazir Malikev in the private parts.'

'What on earth for?'

'He said some terrible things.'

'What things my Balim?'

'About you. That you are a traitor…'

And then Gayibova moves round to comfort the girl and she wraps her arms round her and kisses her head.'

'Two minutes.' I call out to the far side of the room and they both look over at me as if they have seen me for the first time. And again, I feel how shameful it is to envy a condemned woman.

Once the daughter has departed, we walk back to the cell: her, three strides ahead, me behind dragging the useless foot along with the familiar thump swish rhythm on the dusty floor. All the cells are quiet. Just the occasional rustle and shady movement in the black corners where the rats scuttle.

I unlock the door to the cell and light the flame in the paraffin lamp on the shelf.

'You didn't tell her?'

'No,' she sighs.

'Why not?'

'She will find out soon enough. And maybe…'

'No. No maybe.'  I press some fresh tobacco into the pipe bowl and light it from the lamp with a taper.

'So, what do you want? For your last meal?' I ask her but she stares for a long while through the window and I think she is not going to answer.

'Plov' she says after some moments.

'Fine. That's easy. Rice and meat.' In the lamp glow her eyes glint like a blade betrayed behind a robber's back.

'With apricots and roast chestnuts from Taza Bazaar. Oh, and halva for dessert. And some Azeri wine.'

So still the old spark then. I have tried my best to choke it but, like the tiny blaze on Fire Mountain, it seems unquenchable and perpetual.

She seats herself at the desk, staring out into nothing. Her back as straight as a flagpole, her torso sways to a silent rhythm, dipping and straightening as though possessed by something supernatural and her fingers dance like dervishes upon the battered wooden desk. She is composing a new tune: a brand-new tune to sing at dawn.

# EYES ON THE MOON

## VALERIE HOARE

"This can't be happening."

Her voice startled me, she sounded disbelieving, angry. I'd been waiting in silence, almost dozing, for ten minutes. I'd listened to the wind hurl itself around the wooden shelter, rattling the clear side panels.

"What's that?" I asked.

She looked at me, her face was very pale. I saw fear in her eyes.

"Sorry, I didn't mean to speak out loud," she said.

Her voice was raspy, like her throat was sore.

I've never been one to hold my tongue, it's not in my nature. And anyway, I know how people see me. I'm just a nosy old woman.

"Can I help?"

She looked at me again, then as if deciding I was probably harmless, she slid along the seat until she was a little closer. Her eyes were dark green pools, teary and wide. She looked out to sea silently.

The promenade was nearly empty; the few people who passed us were dog walkers, hurrying to get out of the cold. It wasn't the time of year for the seaside. A large gull drifted in on the wind and landed heavily in front of the shelter. It looked at me, eye to eye.

"He came home today," she said abruptly. "My fiance, Ryan. He's in the Navy."

"That's lovely, isn't it?"

She shook her head. Her auburn hair fell loose from its clips as she did but she didn't notice. It was beginning to get dark; the winter sun set early. I could just see the ships passing on the horizon as I looked out to sea, like tiny bath toys in the distance. In another five minutes the light would be gone completely. The gull waited, hoping for scraps.

"I promised to be there to meet him," she said, then burst into tears.

Her shoulders shook but she made no sound. I moved closer and tried to take her hand. It was very cold, I noticed, before she pulled away from me.

"You mustn't get too close, I might still be infectious."

Her look told me she knew the drill.

"You don't have a mask," she said.

"Don't fret, I'm immune."

"Still, it's risky," she warned, "you can't be sure."

I've worn enough masks in my time, one way and another, to know they don't always help, or hide. But I didn't argue, I moved away from her.

"Why can't you meet him?" I asked.

"I've been ill, I can't risk giving it to him."

"Can't you call him? Everyone has a pocket telephone now, don't they?"

She frowned at me, confused, then patted her pockets.

I may have said the wrong thing, used the wrong words. I do that sometimes.

"I had one," she said, "but they must've taken it away." She sniffed back the tears that threatened to start again.

"Well, he'll come to find you, won't he? If he cares for you?"

She nodded.

"But I won't be there," she said sadly. Her face scrunched up as she collapsed in tears again. This time she couldn't hold back, she let out a wail of grief.

I looked around, alarmed. But there was no one about to hear, only the gull.

"There, now," I said, reaching out to hold her close. She didn't resist.

"What's your name?" I asked, hoping to calm her.

"Kaylee," she stammered.

"I'm Rose."

I held her, noticing her bony shoulders, even through her thick coat. She shivered as a gust of wind swirled off the sea into the shelter. I don't seem to feel the cold anymore, not like I used to. My coat's not as thick as hers but it was all I could get when I bought it and it's old now. The gull wandered off in search of supper.

"Why won't you be there, it's quite close, isn't it, where the ships come in?"

She nodded but still shuddered with each sob that overtook her.

I knew she was probably the one I'd been sent to fetch, the directions aren't usually far wrong. Why else would I be sitting in a seafront shelter in winter? But to be sure, I needed her to answer me properly.

"Is there something else wrong with you," I asked plainly.

Her voice was a whisper.

"Yes."

She looked straight at me, as if trying to make up her mind about something.

"You'll think I'm crazy," she said at last.

I suppose there could be another reason why she was here now, another good excuse. But the empty feeling coming from her made me think she was the one. I tried a different tack.

"I was meant to meet my young man here, years ago, when he came back from the war." I hadn't spoken about that time for too long, I'd tried not to think of it.

There was a spell of complete quiet then, the wind dropped away and no people passed. In the dark sky a few scattered stars appeared, pinheads of light.

Kaylee was watching my face, I felt her eyes on me.

"Which war was that?' she asked suspiciously. "My granddad was in the last big one, and he died when I was at school. It can't have been then, I'm not stupid."

My mind wanted to relive the awful days, I had to drag myself back.

"No, not that one. The Great War, 1914 to 1918." I hardly knew my voice, I sounded really young again. I let the memory pull me in.

"That's even further back," she said. "You can't be that old."

I smiled at her. In my head I was still Rose, the volunteer nurse. Kaylee's probably older now than I was then.

Gilbert was away, like all the young men, facing the

unimaginable. I had no idea if he would come back, the least I could do was help the wounded lads who did. I couldn't tell Kaylee about Grace, though.

We were nursing together, me and Grace, at the Cottage hospital. We got very close.

She was different from the other girls I knew, solid and determined, sure of what she wanted. Before I knew it, I was in love with her. I'd never even thought of another girl in that way before.

She felt the same for me, she said. She asked me to promise I'd be hers alone. She had no doubts about our future but I was torn. I couldn't just drop Gilbert, though, not while he was away. I couldn't be that cruel, I loved him too.

Grace and I shared everything for months: our food, our work, our happy moments. Our love. We had to keep that secret, no-one knew. I still wrote to Gilbert but his letters back were few. I began to think he might not come home.

Kaylee was watching me, I could see the curiosity on her face. I had to shake my memories aside again.

"Some days I look younger than others," I said, "but I am that old, really."

I waited for her to take that in, perhaps she was doing the sums in her head.

"What was his name?" she asked.

"Gilbert."

She'd stopped crying now, I'd got her attention. I went on.

"He went to France, doing his duty. I was proud of him but scared he'd be killed."

Kaylee held my hand tight now, the worry of infection had faded.

"Did he die?" She spoke quietly, I think she'd started to see the point of my story.

"No, he made it home, just like we'd dreamed of," I answered slowly, remembering.

"But…"

"But I wasn't there to meet him."

I looked at her young face and saw myself.

"We had a sickness then, too, Kaylee," I said, "every bit as bad as this one and we didn't know how to stop it."

That was when the hospital was overtaken by the Spanish Flu, I remembered. The soldiers came back with it and it soon spread to us nurses. Grace got ill first. I was frantic, trying to tend to her and the other patients at the same time. She was young, strong and healthy before but it didn't help. She only lasted two days. She died holding my hand one windy night, still telling me how she loved me.

I hadn't lasted long without Grace. By the end of the week I was sick too. I asked them to write to Gilbert, to tell him. I think they did but the letter never reached him. I was long gone when he came home.

It was getting hard to keep my mind on my work. I'd drifted back to the old days again and had to remember why I was in the shelter now.

"I caught the Flu and—"

"You didn't survive." Kaylee finished my sentence.

I nodded, sad now at the memory.

"Like me," she said simply.

I smiled at her.

"Like you. You understand it's time to go, don't you?"

She nodded.

"I didn't want to believe it. That's why I came out here. I

thought if I could meet Ryan, like we promised, it would mean I was going to be ok."

Her green eyes were wide again with the shocking memory.

"He couldn't see me, he walked straight past. Then I knew."

I had to force my mind back to Kaylee and her story. I wouldn't tell her how I had struggled at first to accept my fate. I remembered how much it hurt. I still wouldn't share my other secret either, even after so long, not everyone would understand that. I wanted to reassure her, to comfort her but time was short. I was under orders.

I've seen Grace, and Gilbert, a few times since we went up. But we all have our jobs and our places to be. It's not always easy to be where we'd like. I pushed down my longing.

"It'll be alright, you'll see. Look at me, I've come through so many years. It's not so bad really, you just have to adjust and relax.

Kaylee stood and pulled me up from the hard seat.

"I can't change it, can I?" She sounded bold, resigned now.

"No, it's done."

She tucked her arm through mine. I felt the warmth of her touch through my sleeve.

"Where do we go?" she said. "Show me the way."

"Just keep your eyes on the moon and let yourself fly," I said.

# BIDDEN

## RICHARD HOOTON

The maître d' bows as I pass through The Holly's arched doorway. I've a spring in my step as we curve the circular bar that dominates the dining room's centre. Yesterday's news was a real fillip. And Emily was on top form last night.

'This way please, Mr Lavender.'

Air conditioning circulates a cool breeze and the tantalising aroma of roasted meats and spices. Well-heeled customers, sitting on stools upholstered in red leather, glance at me. I push my shoulders back. Gershwin's Rhapsody in Blue frolics in the background. We reach a table in the corner, overlooking the room. The maître d' gives a theatrical arm swoop.

Roger Merrell's already seated. Always first. Likes to give the impression you've kept him waiting. He stands. His navy suit is cut to perfection. Lean but jowly, a firmly knotted tie keeps loose folds of skin tucked under his shirt. I've never seen him dressed informally; brogues always polished. It makes me conscious of my open collar attire, just as his close shave makes my five o'clock shadow feel like stubble.

Roger holds out a paw, flashing whitened teeth.

'Secretary of State.' His sandpaper timbre fails to scrape the shine from the words. 'How good of you to join me.'

Well, he did summon me. Ministers used to control these media moguls. Now he's nicknamed Geppetto. Knowledge is power.

His handshake is vice tight and vigorous.

The maître d' pulls out a chair. I sit and he drapes a linen napkin over my lap. Roger whispers something in the maître d's ear, sending him on his way. Then retakes his seat, ramrod straight as a soldier. I smile at my host in the same way I do for his photographer's cameras: a fixed but uneasy grin.

'To what do I owe the pleasure, Roger?'

There's always a catch.

'Haven't seen you for so long, Jason.' From a certain angle, his wide smile makes him resemble a shark. 'And to celebrate your promotion.'

It's taken forever to climb the ladder to the high office of Business Secretary. Years of campaigning and lobbying, endless meetings and constituents' complaints. Clambering and clinging to each rung; from sitting on select committees to bag carrying for the dourest of Ministers.

'Always good to see you, Roger.'

Particularly as he owns four national newspapers and is the major shareholder and CEO of a satellite TV company.

Attached to the restaurant's dark wooden panelling are Victorian portraits of the leading gentlemen in their fields: finance, medicine, literature. Moustached men in bowler hats, cravats and waistcoats. I feel a sense of belonging, the radiance of accomplishment, to be part of this esteemed company.

A pretty, gazelle-like waitress approaches carrying a bottle of wine. She presents it to Roger as if it's jewellery before pouring an inch of deep ruby into a glass. Roger gives it a swirl. Sips.

'Good.'

The opinion is instant. The waitress fills our glasses solemnly. She positions the bottle on our table. A 1998 Château Haut-Brion, a grand classic; will have set Roger back a four-figure sum. Should I be flattered, or frightened?

The waitress sashays past. I can't resist a glance at her derrière. Turning back, I find Roger watching me. His pugilistic face has more crests and crevices than a mountain landscape. Large, wire-rimmed spectacles seem designed to cover every angle of vision.

'How's business?' I ask, smoothing my napkin.

His green eyes flit, taking in whatever's happening behind me. 'Difficult,' he growls. 'The board has differences of opinion.'

I lift my glass by the stem. The nose soars with rich, ripe blackberries and blueberries. I sip. Full-bodied, perfect balance and harmony on the palate. Notes of smoke and cherry liqueur in the finish. Delightful.

'I need that controlling stake. If you…'

I raise an open-palmed hand. 'You know I can no longer discuss that with you, Roger.'

Legal restrictions constrain media ownership. But only a takeover referred to the regulators by the Business Secretary will be scrutinised. I cannot be seen to be influenced.

Roger's face stiffens. It feels as though the air conditioning has stopped. I glance around. The quirky stained glass windows let colourful diamonds of light cascade over us while shielding our presence from those outside.

The waitress bestows us with bowls: a light green consommé containing floating vegetation, rather reminiscent of my duck pond.

'I took the liberty of ordering for us.' Roger holds his spoon like a baton.

The waitress stares at me. I tilt my head, eyebrows raised. 'Fancy a photo, dear?'

She averts her gaze. Scampers away.

A careful sup. The pea flavour at least has a refreshing mintiness.

'It's *my* company.' Roger slurps rapid spoonfuls. 'I built it, it's *mine* by rights.' He has no regard for the required manners. 'It's unfair, undignified, to be blocked from owning it outright.'

The restaurant's busy but has sufficient space between tables to *not* be overheard. Media ownership has long been politically controversial. Even some of my colleagues agree with the opposition's view that freedom of speech is enhanced by a plurality and diversity of editorial voices. It won't do to get dragged into an argument.

'I simply cannot discuss it.' I smile in the way I do to my wife when averting a quarrel. 'More than my job's worth.'

Roger knows full well that the idea of one man controlling a large proportion of our nation's newspaper and broadcasting interests is of huge public concern. Especially when that person takes such a close interest in his organisation's political agenda – and claims to be able to sway elections.

Roger finishes his soup with a clattering spoon. I'm half-way through.

'It's unfortunate your predecessor had to resign.' He wipes his mouth with his napkin. 'But we had a duty to publish those stories.'

Heat prickles my neck. I don't need reminding that the previous minister blocked his takeover bid – and paid a heavy price: career, marriage and family collapsing around him.

'Yes, very unfortunate.' Still, Vernon was foolish to declare war openly on Roger in a doomed bid to shore up liberal support. 'Though everyone's *entitled* to a private life.'

'A private life is what people want when they've done something wrong.'

I finish my starter in silence. The waitress returns, pouring more wine with enough tremble to spill some, a growing red stain sullying the tablecloth's white linen.

'Careful, girl.' Roger glares at her. 'Have you any idea how much each drop of that costs?'

'So sorry, Sir.' Her cheeks redden. She collects the bowls. Scurries off.

Roger's features settle into thought. I know better than to interrupt. I enjoy the wine. Mustn't let it go to my head. Light chatter flows around us, the occasional guffaw. Roger never laughs.

'How's the wife?'

'Very well, thank you. Sends her love.'

'Been married, what, twenty years?'

I nod while noticing a sweet little brass lamp on the table; so preferable to the long-burning candles they used to have, which end up a molten mess.

'Must have been teenagers when you tied the knot.' That smile is more dazzling than the cutlery.

'You're too kind, Roger.' I run a hand through my hair. 'Mid-twenties.'

The waitress serves our main course. Roger wields his steak knife, carving through the sirloin to expose flesh pink to the point of bloody.

'Ahh.' Roger scrutinises it. 'Rare like me.' He chews on a large chunk. 'And the kids?'

The tender meat cuts easily. 'Xander's studying for GCSEs. Sophia thinks only of horses.'

'Family matters.' Juice squirts from an heirloom tomato that Roger's slicing.

The wine matches the steak perfectly. 'They mean everything to me.'

Roger skewers a piece of meat. 'Along with the job.'

'Especially the job.'

Roger's quick with the knife. He's almost devoured his steak. 'How's that new parliamentary assistant of yours doing?'

That heat returns, my neck febrile. I take a swallow of wine, it does go down very easily. 'Emily's performing brilliantly.' I sample a triple-cooked chip, crisp and fluffy. 'She's a bright young thing.'

'Heard a lot about that girl. She'll go far.'

Best change the subject. 'How's your family?'

'Good.' Roger pauses. 'Keeping in line.' He consumes his last piece of meat. 'Jack's got some liberal ideas, bit disconcerting. Sawyer's a chip off the old block.'

I feel the cool relief of a stricken pilot reaching safe

ground. 'No thoughts of retirement?' Must be in his seventies now. His sons will be jockeying for position.

A bemused look. 'Work is my life, Jason.'

I hadn't noticed the waitress lingering. 'Is everything to your satisfaction…' – she carefully tops up our glasses – '…gentlemen?'

Roger bats her away like a gnarled lion with a fly.

'I've done a huge amount of good for this country. Bringing business and employment, investment and innovation. Keeping newspapers going, giving people a choice of channels and quality programmes.'

He's certainly created an empire. His parents were nothing special – father a GP, mother a teacher. His father ruled with an iron rod, I'm told. Roger worked his way up through the newspaper industry until he could afford to own a local rag, then branched out, buying and selling. Eventually, he went national, snapping up titles.

'And now I'm not even allowed to control what's *mine*.'

Must be more than thirty years since Thatcher's government allowed him to take over two broadsheets without referring it to the Monopolies and Merger Commission, even though he already owned two tabloids. An unprecedented merger rushed through in three days over fears the newspapers could close. A decision hotly criticised in Parliament and press. I later learnt the Minister at the time had been minded to refer, then mysteriously changed his mind. Roger's now stronger than ever. And still wanting more.

'Can't you be satisfied with what you already have?'

He looks at me as if I'm speaking Japanese. What drives him? When so many men his age would be happy to sit back and enjoy the fruits of their success. Hard not to admire him really.

Leaning back, I quaff my wine, savouring its heady glow. Wonder if Emily's available tonight?

A steely-eyed stare. 'How's the wife?'

He's already asked after Susan. For a moment, I hope it's a sign of forgetfulness. Possibly even the onset of dementia. But no. His mind remains razor sharp. An edge to the tone, a disconcerting twinkle in his eye. Sweat troubles my brow. Now I know where we're going. Or rather, where he's taking me.

I gulp some wine. It can't drown the bad taste in my mouth.

'Susan's well.' My tone is flat.

I glance at the paintings. An anxious Victorian glowers back. I push the remnants of my meal around my plate.

Roger scrunches his napkin. 'I'm not having a dessert. Don't like anything sweet.' He downs his drink. 'You help yourself, Jason.' A glance at his Rolex. 'Got to get going – another meeting at eight. I've already settled the bill. Don't worry about that.'

At the bar, cocktail glasses hang upside down from a brass-tiled ceiling.

'You'll never retire, will you?'

He actually laughs. A deep, throaty chuckle. 'I'll keep buggering on until I drop, Jason. Then Sawyer will keep my legacy going.' Roger stands. 'Family matters.'

'I couldn't agree more,' I mutter.

'Knew we'd understand each other.' Roger slaps me on the back. 'Congratulations again. You'll go far.'

I feel the echoing sting of his hand, like its presence remains. I flinch as if pulled by strings.

'Nothing escapes me, Jason.' Roger strolls away.

'Anything else?' The waitress looms over me with a sour expression. What's she overheard?

I shake my head.

'Thought I recognised you.' She stares at my wedding ring, nose wrinkling. 'I know Emily.'

I open my mouth. Think again.

She looks at Roger's empty chair. 'And his rival editor who dines here.'

Snorting, I toss my napkin onto my messy plate.

A smile dawns on her face. She sets about cleaning up the disorder.

My mind spinning with headlines, I trudge back down to Westminster.

# LOVE CONQUERS ALL

## DON HORNE

Drool slides from the corner of dad's mouth, his hand quivering near his chin, failing to dab it away. I gently guide him, struggling to contain my feelings as his helpless look guts me.

*Must keep things positive, for his sake.*

"Let's make you more comfortable eh?" as I reach behind him for the square patchwork cushion, summer colours of yellow, blue and green, recalling mum's snippy reaction when I bought it years ago, "Wasted money Kate. I could have run up something for you."  I came to realise her upbringing was guided by parents who lived frugal and uneventful lives, and she struggled to find a passion in hers.

The cushion is keeping pace with dad, squashed, and colours dull, lacking lustre.  Bang it like a concertina.  Fluff it. I draw him forward into a happy cuddle, kissing his forehead, taking in the citrus notes of his *Old Spice* aftershave.

*Am I applying it after every shave to keep things normal, or is it denial of what lies ahead?*

Wrap my arms around him, silently pleading with some supernatural power to repel the disabilities and give him back to me. Finally, ease him back into the cushion's softness, "That'll be better for you Dad." His watery blue eyes find mine and he gives a little nod, a gentle smile pulling down the right side of his mouth.

Our lounge room is ice-box cool after an overnight low. Morning clouds have been banished by thin afternoon sun pushing through the coloured leadlight windows, creating red, green, purple and yellow shapes on the pale walls, just as I've always loved. Little girl memories I still treasure, using the patterns as backdrops for my make-believe stories. Fairies and nymphs dancing in a sunlit glade.

China cups and saucers are set on a delicate white lace tablecloth with a rose pattern. My own work and from my collection.  Settling alongside him I pour tea from the matching china teapot, the way he likes it. Leaf not bags, his constant reminder back in our good days, *Let it draw for three minutes Kate to get the rich flavour. Never use a metal pot. China for best result, Pumpkin.*

I lift the cup and he takes a sip, his left hand wrapping mine, feeling like sandpaper, papery-thin skin drying so quickly in this climate. Have I been so pre-occupied with my own problems that I've neglected his moisturiser? Another sip, and another.  It's just right because he doesn't hold it in his mouth, cheeks puffed before swallowing like when I make it with tea bags – to let me know I can't get one past him, despite his stroke and weakening heart.

Afternoon tea over, I clear the china from the table. Can tell he enjoyed a date scone, freshly made from the oven, and most of his tea.  I remove his messy bib, splattered with blackberry jam from his scone, and check his bag to make sure it doesn't need emptying. Finally, adjust his lazy-boy so he can comfortably watch the telly. It's Saturday and he's not into football, so I scan the apps for police dramas, things he can attempt to follow of sorts.  "How about *Midsomer Murders*? OK?"

I get a twisted smile and his best attempt at a nod. His effort pulls me to him for another hug and kiss.

As I start *Midsomer* he gives a few shivers, so I fetch a soft mohair rug from my old camphor wood chest, to wrap around him. The chest was supposed to be a Glory Box for my married life, but now consigned to a corner of our back room with just a few things remaining. My special collection progressively found its way into everyday use as my hope for a wedding slipped away with each passing year.

Every day dad seems to be shrinking before my eyes, a frail reminder of the robust man I cherished. Looks older than his years. Long ago as a little girl I'd spend cold days snuggled in his lap while he read me stories.  Can still feel the soft wool of his sweaters or rough tweed of jackets on my arms and legs. Remember my fingers finding their way to the buttons on his vest, undoing and redoing them, and how he'd return my little hands to my lap. *Don't leave dirty marks Pumpkin.*

Dad was the reader, not my mother. We'd settle in his comfy lounge chair with my books, evenings and at weekends when he wasn't working. Special treats were *Possum Magic* and visits to the bookshop, holding my hand as I looked for any new books from Mem Fox.

Sewing and knitting were mum's things. Thankfully, she taught me embroidery and this became my hobby as a girl.

The faded cushion on the lounge is a reminder that I was rather good at it once. Each cursive letter, neat and tidy, against a lemon background, surrounded by blue forget-me-nots.

I tuck his hands under the mohair rug. It is soft, light, and will keep him warm on this chilly afternoon. Can't afford the heater so early, just managing on his pension, a care plan and my benefits. The next hour or so will give me time to tidy the house and tackle a basket of ironing while I keep an eye on him. And to prepare for the unavoidable talk I must face.

———

"Didn't hear you come in last night. What time was it?" my mother on her usual twenty questions after my date.

"A little after ten," catching dad's small wink, knowing it was later.

"Are you seeing him again?"

"How are you feeling Mum?"

"Don't answer my question with a question. It doesn't wash. Now are you seeing him again?"

"No Mum."

"And why not this time?"

"He has bad breath."

"Oh for goodness sakes Kate, stop being so pernickety. Way too fussy, finding fault with everyone. Last time it was *too short for me*. Before that *doesn't know how to use his knife and fork properly*. Next thing it'll be *he has false teeth*. As I keep saying, time's slipping away my girl. And good men with it. At 33 you aren't a spring chicken you know."

"Get off her back Maggie. It'll happen one day. Sometimes

I think you don't want it to happen anyway." Dad, full of sympathy, fixes on me not my mother.  My smile sends him a thank you.

She bluntly tells him it's women's territory.

"Not much chance though for her to get into a relationship Maggie, with her tied to your apron strings. Some fellas would run a mile from that."

"That's unfair Geoff.  Don't know what I'd do without Kate, what with my health problems. All this talk has set my nerves off again."

I help her back into bed, propped up with two pillows.

"Could you get my book Kate, and another cup of tea please? You know I'd fall apart without you. Sit for a minute and I'll tell you what has to be done today."

Clutching her list I return to the kitchen.

"Ease your bones into a chair Pumpkin." Dad gently closes the door and sits facing me, "I know I've said this many times but I'll say it again for what it's worth. It's high time you moved out on your own while we're still able to manage. You have your own life to live.  She's clinging to you. Don't let time slip away."

I walk around the table and wrap my arms around him, holding him tightly, "I love you so much Dad."

"Love you too Pumpkin. But think about it. Make the break. We can cope."

*Am I staying because she needs me, or because I want to look after him?*

————

Across the room I watch dad moving around, thanking people for coming to mum's funeral. He was unshakeable about her care, "My parents had unhappy lives in a nursing home. Too many bad memories. No way your mother's going there." We shared her care at home.

Now free of all her on-call attention, it's like I'm seeing dad in real time. I'm startled, with a feeling that I'm re-appearing in his life, despite being here all the time. He looks so much older. Slower in his movements and hair almost silver. Deeper lines in his face and cheeks hollowing out. His changes have silently passed me by, not touching the sensors of my awareness and concern.

*Dear Dad I'm with you now.*

I move to his side, linking my arm through his, as he continues to work the room with his gracious appreciation of people's support. We pass the big mirror hanging above the sideboard and I catch my reflection. Curly salt and pepper hair, cut simply for comfort, not for style. Glasses hiding my green eyes, and minimal make-up doing nothing for my face which is also showing its share of lines. My mother's words fill my mind as we move to another group in the crowded room.

Detective Chief Inspector Barnaby puts the suspect behind bars in *Midsomer* and I turn off the telly. Dark clouds have replaced the sunshine, dusk clearing the rainbow colours from the room. I switch on the overhead pendant light to dispel the gloom. Dad looks uncomfortable so I ease him out of his lazy-boy for a gentle exercise walk arm-in-arm around the room. As we pass the coffee table I reach down and pick up my fine lace cloth draping it over my head like a veil, pretending we are walking down the aisle.

"Who gives this woman's hand in holy matrimony, eh Dad?" I feel him straighten and his good hand finds mine. He turns to my mother's photo on the sideboard. Tears come to my eyes as I hear a muffled attempt at "Maggie."

Our make-believe comes to an end alongside his chair. With his special twisted smile he attempts to lift my hand and offer it to a waiting bridegroom. I kiss him and ease him into his chair as though it's a pew in the church.

Removing the veil I move my chair so I can face him while I explain what's about to happen. I take his hands and look into his watery eyes, "Don't know how to say this any other way."

A quick slur, like "I know," with a small nod.

"It's time for a painful decision, Dad," squeezing his hands for reassurance and feeling a gentle response. Is it my imagination I wonder; is he reading my mind, willing me on? Maybe my bulky sweaters and over-dressing haven't fooled him about my progressive weight loss?

Gather strength for what I'm about to tell him. Try my best to stop trembling, "I need to go into hospital. Something to do with my pancreas. Doctors are a bit concerned."

*Can't tell him that I've been advised to prepare for the worst, and to get my affairs in order.*

Another squeeze of my hand.

"It will mean separation," hugging him tightly to hide the fear that must be filling my face. I hold back tears, "We'll find a nice, comfortable place for you, and talk more about it tomorrow."

*My mind is a slide-show of his life ahead, budgeted care from unfamiliar faces, in a room off a clinical corridor. No family support. Another name in a managed system. Against all his wishes.*

I lower his lazy-boy, easing him back, tucking the rug around him and start the heater to warm the room. "Have a little sleep Dad while I start getting tea ready."

When his breathing becomes regular and I'm sure he's sleeping, I quietly collect my lemon cushion from the lounge and place it over his face, pressing down until I'm sure he's no longer breathing, staring at my carefully embroidered cursive letters, *Love Conquers All*, surrounded by blue forget-me-nots.

# FINGER GUNS

## SEÁ MCNICHOLL

The bombs changed everything.

That's when Mammy became petrified of us being killed.

Don't get me wrong, she had always been worried about it; that's just how life was in Belfast in the early Seventies. But after the car bombs went off on Bloody Friday, she changed.

Shrapnel and blood painted the streets, and she shipped us off to her sister Elizabeth in South Armagh.

As if that was any safer.

She didn't seem to realise it was out of the frying pan and into the fire.

"The Fenians will have the town destroyed, better off hiding amongst them out in the sticks," my father had said.

Christ, I fought tooth and nail to stay. I really did.

Belfast was my town, my land, my home. I wanted to fight to defend it, to defend our people and to defend the Crown, whatever that meant. Politics is difficult to understand when you're eight. But I knew the Crown was ours and not theirs.

The old men had told me so. We were right and they were Fenians. I wanted to stay.

But as a child your voice isn't heard. Or it's ignored. Either way, I was packed into the back of Aunty Lizzie's Kadett and brought out to the country, to the wild.

Now bear in mind, as a boy of eight I had never left Belfast. The only cow I'd ever seen was in a school book. So to me, South Armagh seemed a magical place – a vast expanse of rolling green hills, hugged by rivers and streams that consummated in lakes and loughs. The Belfast streets and the Crown were soon forgotten.

In the back of Aunty Lizzie's Kadett, I had been transplanted into a fairytale; south Armagh in late July.

Country folk aren't like city folk. I'd say that's true across the world. Different surroundings birth different cultures. And Aunty Lizzie and Mammy couldn't have been further apart. Mammy was a well prune cherry blossom girded by metal rings, Aunt Lizzy was a wild oak with branches vast and unruly.

At home, we would be allowed to play in our street, and in our street only, under the watchful eye of many's a mammy. Beyond our street a Fenian might grab us.

But in south Armagh, Aunty Lizzie would harry me out the door, calling after to "only come home when you're lost."

And so it was, me the Belfast boy out to find my adventure in a fairytale. Truth be told, it was a slow start. The back garden was enough of an adventure at the beginning; I was still a city boy after all. But as the days crept to weeks, so my daring grew and soon neither fence nor brier could hold me.

I traversed ravines and forded streams. I saved damsels from their ash-tree towers and chased invisible villains down badger setts with my stick-ish rapier. I sailed the Atlantic as blue waves crashed amongst the golden barley fields, and I shot at German soldiers hiding amongst the flocks of sheep.

Until one day a stranger stood in the midst of my fairytale.

"Who are you?" he asked bluntly.

It's a wonder how small talk isn't necessary amongst children.

He startled me, and I squinted into the early morning sun to see him. He was about my height, maybe a bit taller if I'm remembering him rightly, and he gave me a blank stare.

"Billy Anderson," I answered.

"That sounds like a Proddy name," he replied, "you a Prod?"

"I think so," I said. I knew I was Presbyterian though I wasn't sure if that made me a *Prod*. Some of the older kids on the street had said that's what the Fenians called us. So I guessed I was a Prod.

"Really!?" he said excitedly, eyes widening, "I've never seen a Prod before! 'Cept for Paisley on the telly. You sorta talk like him too. Where are you from?"

I didn't know who Paisley was, but I wondered if he was a Presbyterian.

"Belfast."

"Wow," he said, bouncing on his heel with eyes alight, "A Proddy from Belfast!" I didn't know how to answer so I just looked at my now-grass-stained shoes. The wee boy thought for a moment, looking down on me, probing – studying, like I was an unseen bug beneath his magnifying glass.

"Why are you here?"

I shrugged the reply, wanting to scuttle beneath the leaves

to safety. "Mammy thought it was too dangerous in Belfast with the bombs."

"Does she not know there's bombs here too?" he asked me as he braved a step closer.

I shrugged again and he straightened and nodded.

"My name's Pearse Murphy." He said it formally, sticking out his hand like the old men did. I shook it, as men do.

He wrinkled his brow as he scanned the sun-touched horizon behind me.

"You'd need to watch yourself," he attempted to mutter like an old man too, "there's not many Prods 'round here. Is your Mammy here?"

I shook my head.

"Is she dead?"

I shook harder. "She sent me live with my Aunty Lizzie."

He thought for a moment and then nodded. He knew who she was.

"So is your daddy in the Brits?"

"No. He works in a factory." I answered.

"Oh," he said, his nose scrunching, "I thought all Prods were in the Brits."

"I don't think they're the same thing," I said, but in truth I wasn't sure. I didn't know exactly what a Prod was. "The Brits wear army clothes and carry guns. My daddy wears old clothes and doesn't have a gun."

"My daddy has a gun!" The boy exclaimed excitedly. "My daddy's in the Provos! And when I grow up, I'm going to be in the IRA too and I'll be the head of the IRA and I'll drive the Brits out and I'll free Ireland!"

He pulled out finger guns and started shooting wildly.

"But the IRA are bad guys," I answered as fear crept

across me. He must be a bad boy. Fenians are the baddies. They don't like the Crown.

"No they're not!" he said, his cheeks flaring to battle, "You're the bad guys! The Prods and the Brits!"

"But you blew up Belfast and killed all those people!" I said trying to stifle a childish sob, like many children do when faced with confrontation they don't understand.

"But you shot way more! You shot all those men in Derry and they were just marching. Didn't have guns or nothing. And you just shot them. Pew! Pew! Pew!"

He fired at me.

I was barely holding back tears now as I cried, "I didn't!"

He held a ceasefire and holstered his finger guns.

"You don't need to cry," he said to the ground as he pushed a stone under his toe.

In fairytales, heroes and villains don't fall into awkward silences or wonder where to put their eyes. I started to wonder if this was a fairytale land or just a dark, foreboding fable.

"My uncle was shot by the Brits," he said quietly, still focusing on the stone beneath his shoe. "Have any of your ones been killed?"

He flicked his eyes up.

I nodded.

"My uncle was blown up in Tyrone. He worked for the BBC."

Rays of fear spread across me as a realisation began to dawn.

"Where's your daddy?" I asked quickly, looking round, expecting to find myself staring down the nozzle of a gun.

Pearse had lost interest in the stone and was now kicking at dandelions.

"Long Kesh," he said as he lifted a yellow head from the stalk with a swift swipe.

"Where's that?"

"You know, the jail? Where they sent all the daddies last year."

I frowned.

"My daddy isn't in Long Kesh," I said nervously.

He shrugged his answer.

"All the daddies around here are. All the Catholic daddies. The Brits turned up in the middle of the night and took them all away."

My daddy was at home. He wasn't in Long Kesh. None of the daddies in my street were in Long Kesh.

"Did he kill someone?" I asked.

It's a wonder how tact isn't necessary amongst children.

The rest of the dandelions were spared as Pearse tore his attention from them.

"Do you want to go see my treehouse?" he asked, running the sleeve of his jumper across his eyes.

"Ok," I replied and we set off together across the field where I had said the Atlantic, saved the damsels and shot the hidden German soldiers.

And so we spent the summer as two boys should, out in a make believe world , a world we crafted together, far from reality under the south Armagh sun.

Some days the treehouse would be the centre of operations as we fought off invisible cowboys with their six-shooters, other days it was our home as a violent storm threatened to blow it away underneath a clear blue sky. We crossed continents within the span of a few hundred yards and touched down on the moon by the river's bank.

Our only time spent as enemies was when we were cops and robbers and our little finger guns sought each other as one tried to escape with the loot.

He showed me things not known to the old men of Belfast; the cry of a pheasant startled by young huntsmen, the sanctity of the fairy tree, the clotted slobber of frogspawn as young fingers probed. My mind was opened to a new world that summer. A world that, at the time, seemed to stretch into eternity beneath the late summer sun.

But all worlds and eternities end when you're a child. My own was harkened by the hum of a Kadett engine ready to take me back to the September streets of Belfast and another school year.

Our goodbyes were brief and void of sorrow, as they should be to a child, too young to understand parting.

"Bye."

"Bye bye."

Simple words and a wave as the car door closed on our young friendship.

And soon Pearse and his world was just a story about "What I Did This Summer" that I would tell my teacher and classmates about.

Twelve summers had come and passed before I heard of Pearse again, the bombs and bullets ever more frequent, the furrows of division deepened by the rains of hatred; Belfast in the 1980s.

I was a passenger in my father's Ford Cortina as we headed home from another dry day at the factory, the radio droning just above the engine. He highered it up as he did every day when the repetitive bleeps announced the beginning of the news.

"Welcome to BBC Radio Ulster, it's six o'clock, the headlines. An IRA gunman has been shot dead in south Armagh. The custom workers' strike continues into a third day. And Allied Carpets has been damaged again in a bomb attack."

I continued to pick at the dirt that had crawled beneath my nails. Same old life. Same old news.

"The RUC have confirmed an IRA gunman has been shot dead outside Cullyhanna in South Armagh. The incident happened when a vehicle refused to stop at an army checkpoint. The assailant was shot as he attempted to flee. He has been named locally as Pearse Murphy. The trade union leader for the custom workers-"

My heart dropped at the mention of his name. I stopped picking.

I looked to my father as he grunted something under his breath that sounded like "good riddance." I said nothing.

The sun peeked out from between the clouds, the same sun that shone down on our fairytale summer all those years ago.

A surge of tears threatened as memories of the little boy surfaced.

I looked down at my hands again and holstered my little finger guns.

# HOW TO MURDER A GHOST

DENARII PETERS

I never knew it was possible for a ghost to be as afraid as I am right now.

A shiver passes through me. The words which will end me are being uttered. I can't escape. There is nowhere to go. The man in the chapel, ringing his little bell, waving his book by the light of a guttering candle means me no harm. He wants to free a trapped soul. He believes I am in torment but he is wrong. I don't want to cease to exist but I am already fading. I should never have come to...

———

"...Ackland Hall, ladies and gentlemen, the country seat of Lord and Lady Ackland, reputed to have no less than seven ghosts in residence. One of the most haunted sites in the country, which..."

I tuned out the tour guide's monotonous voice. He had no idea what he was talking about. This house might once have been as he described it but not any longer. It was almost deserted. No, not by the tourists. They come by the coachload to sit in the cafe and eat the scones cooked to "the original Victorian recipe created by Mrs. Grey, the original Victorian cook". Yeah, right. She nipped down to Sainsbury's for them too, did she?

In fact I was the only ghost in the house. Three never existed in the first place, being the inventions of guides over the years, and the remaining three have all been murdered in cold blood by the man in the chapel wielding bell, book and candle.

Yes, I was the last, except... I shouldn't have been there at all. I had answered an advert in Ghosts Abroad. It's an interesting publication. I've consulted it a few times. It lists haunt swaps available throughout the U.K. and Western Europe. The principle is simple. If you get bored with the place where you met your end, you exchange, for a limited period, with another spectre who is just as bored. We spirits have discovered by trial and error that, so long as both the ghosts are agreeable and swap places at the same time, there is no problem. However, you can't go to a place which has no resident ghost and you can't increase the number of ghosts in any location except by more untimely deaths. It's a bit restrictive but it does work.

So, let me tell you about the advert. It had been placed by Lady Josephine Ackland. A spoilt, jilted debutante, she died by hurling herself off the mock battlements of her family's country estate. In the advert she listed the advantages of her place: lovely views, paintings to wobble, pottery to jiggle, draughts available in all main rooms, the perfect haunt for a summer holiday. All I had to offer in exchange was a first floor bedsit with an old, faulty heating system prone to giving off noxious fumes. No dramatic death for me, I'm sorry to say.

I was surprised when she replied to my enquiry at once. She explained that after two hundred plus years of luxury she fancied slumming it for a month or two.

Swap arranged, I told my best friend Sam about it. He was a chimney sweep when the tenement building was a bit grander. He got stuck and starved to death.

He pulled a face, dislodging a few flakes of soot onto the bedsit carpet. I like it when he does that. It confuses the hell out of the current occupant. "There's something odd about Ackland Hall. I saw it in Dead News a few months ago."

"Well, what was it?"

"Can't remember but I think it was about a swap being cancelled at the last minute because the ghost at the hall had suddenly become unavailable for some reason."

I didn't listen. I never do. I was dreaming of drifting round corridors in a long, white dress and standing on the battlements with the wind in my tresses. Lady Josephine had promised me the use of her wardrobe. She was a generous host... or so I thought.

Our swap took place at midnight. They all do and I saw Josephine in passing.

She called out to me, "Sorry about this. Try not to be too upset. It's nothing personal."

I shouted back, "Have a good time. See you in a month."

I arrived at the point from which she had departed. The battlements were rather high. I looked down over the edge but it was too dark and I couldn't see much. I wasn't afraid of falling. A ghost can't be hurt that way. Chances are I would have drifted down as though I were wearing a parachute but

I wasn't about to try it. What I did want was to locate Josephine's wardrobe and get into some more appropriate gear. Who ever heard of an eighteenth century miss wearing Levis?

As I made my way down the grand, central staircase a young girl in a maid's uniform appeared at the bottom.

Her mouth fell open as she caught sight of me. "She did it, didn't she?"

"Hello, I'm Claudia. I'm haunt swapping with..."

"...Lady Josephine. I know but you must go back. You can't stay here. It's..."

She flickered. I can't think of any other way to describe it. She flickered again, becoming ever more transparent, like a breeze blowing through mist.

"Josephine tricked you. There's a... an exorcist..." On the last, terrifying word she gave a howl and was gone.

Shocked, I stared at the empty patch of air. I could hear a faint sound, not her but a chant. Josephine had provided a guide book along with the other paperwork involved in our exchange. I knew where each room was and I had no doubt the sound was coming from the old chapel.

I may not be the most courageous of ghosts but there was nothing for it. I had to find out what was happening.

I passed through the thick, oak door into what should have been an empty stone chamber, the pews and altar having been removed when the chapel was deconsecrated. The first thing I noticed was the acrid stench of sage. The room was strewn with it and bunches of it were suspended either side of a space in the centre. A group of six people knelt there in a rough line in front of a tall, dark haired man. He stood behind a table draped in white linen on top of which were a small brass bell, a large book and a thin, white candle in a silver holder. He wore a thick, grey habit with a hood but I could see the cuffs of jeans and a pair of expensive trainers peeking out from the bottom of it.

"Go to your rest, Eliza!" He beamed at his audience. "It is done. There is now only Lady Josephine Ackland left for us to help on her way. We will reconvene tomorrow at midnight."

His audience scrambled to their feet and left the room.

He began packing his instruments of torture into a holdall. He stopped and looked at me. "I know you're here. I can't see you but I can sense you. I've been a medium since I was born. Tomorrow, I promise I will help you. I will release your unhappy spirit and send you to your eternal rest. Poor, trapped ghost, I will free you."

Poor, trapped ghost? I was, wasn't I? Josephine had conned me into taking her place. I was going to be murdered and there was nothing I could do about it. I would cease to exist.

———

The next morning I tried to contact Ghosts Abroad through the ether but it was the weekend and there was no-one available to help me. I wouldn't be able to leave the building unless I found some other poor sucker to replace me and I wouldn't have done that even if I could.

I watched the tour party as they wandered round with their annoying guide. I had a half baked idea I might be able to find a psychic among them who could intercede. All I did manage to do was irritate a golden retriever who was busy guiding her blind mistress.

The party ate their scones and left.

———

It was five o'clock. In a couple of hours, though I did not want go, I would be drawn to the battlements and have to stay there for a while. It was one of the conditions of the swap. Every day, at the time the event occurred, I had to walk up and down around the spot where Josephine plunged to her death. Would this be the last time anyone did this? With no ghost in residence, Josephine could not return.

Afterwards I drifted through the rooms. I hoped she felt guilty for what she was doing to me.

As midnight approached I went to the chapel. The man was already there, setting up his table and setting out new bunches of sage. Busy, busy.

I plucked at his sleeve but he didn't react. I blew into his face. Nothing happened. He wasn't as psychic as he thought he was. I couldn't get through to him at all. If he knew I was there, he gave no sign of it.

I left the room and went down to the entrance hall. As each of his friends arrived I tried everything I could think of to attract their attention. They shivered with delight as I, frantic with fear, stirred the curtains, chilled them with icy breath and threw pottery from shelves so it smashed at their feet. Only one of them spoke to me and she was facing the wrong direction at the time.

"Oh, sad little ghost, don't worry. Nick will soon release you from your torment."

There was nothing more I could do. My last hope was gone.

The exorcism has begun. I knew the exact moment the chanting started. I was in the drawing room, standing before a portrait of Josephine. I made it fall off the wall but I knew it wasn't damaged. Petty of me but it was all I could do.

Tomorrow the guide will tell his coach party it happened during the night and one of the seven ghosts was responsible. Some of them will go "Ooh!" and some "Ah!". Some will not believe. They will say there are no ghosts at Ackland Hall...

...and they will be right.

# THE UNKINDNESS OF WITCHES

## DENARII PETERS

Could any nightmare have been worse than this?

The angry faces pressed closer, waiting to enjoy my screams but they were going to be disappointed. I would have screamed if I could but there was a rock in my throat. I had thought I could do it. I had been proud of my courage. How self sacrificing. How brave... but it was all gone. If it would have saved me, I would have betrayed Cain. I'd have told them what he had done and where to find him but no-one would listen. They had a witch to burn. That hadn't happened in such a long time.

Nicholas brandished the burning branch. Flames devoured its dried up autumn leaves. I had never liked him. We hadn't been friends and in recent times... Well, I didn't want to think about that. I had never imagined him like this though, his face a rictus grin of pure delight. His was the honour of setting the spark to the tinder around my feet. All I had to do was burn.

One step towards me, urged on with cheers and yells...

one more. I couldn't breathe. I didn't want to burn. I didn't want to die. I had done nothing to deserve this. It hadn't been me.

I closed my eyes. It was so hot, like the hottest day in summer. Crackling, shouting... but where was the pain?

Silence.

I forced my eyes open. Thick smoke billowed. I couldn't see the crowd. Flames leapt up, a curtain of red and yellow but they didn't touch me. There was a tiny gap between me and the fire.

Pressure on my wrists... The rope snaked down around my ankles and charred but didn't burn. The precarious platform of tangled wood on which I was perched felt firmer. I had been sunk to the calves in leaf litter piled up by eager hands. Where had it gone?

My bare feet touched stone. I was surrounded by grey granite walls. The air was cold. I stared around me. I had never imagined I would find myself inside a cave when I died.

Three women faced me.

One held out her hand. "Welcome, sister."

"Where am I?"

"Safe, my dear and among your own kind."

I doubted that. Only one sort of creature could have saved me. These three had to be witches... and I had to get out of there. I wanted to run and fetch help but who would have believed me?

She uttered a string of strange words. Four chairs appeared in the middle of the cave. "Sit down, my dear. You've much to learn. Don't be shy. Tell us your name and show us your talent." She was so pretty for a witch and her voice, oh her voice...

I couldn't help myself. I sat.

"That's better, dear."

"You're witches, aren't you?"

"Oh, what a crude way to describe us... and yourself too. Don't worry. We understand you've had to hide your true nature but that's over now. You needn't be afraid any longer. Do show us everything."

What did they expect of me? They couldn't believe because of where they found me... "You think I'm like you, a witch?" My cheeks flushed at the shame of it. "Is that why you saved me?" My fingers curled round the edge of the chair. What would they do to me when they realised their mistake?

"Relax, my dear. We know you're like us. You can't hide and you no longer have to. I am Hazel. What's your name?"

"I'm called Sophie."

"Tell me more." Her eyes narrowed. Was she annoyed?

Another of them reached out. I couldn't help it. I took her hand. There was a warmth in my fingers, a tingling.

Her eyes held mine. "Your powers are well hidden, sister. My touch is not answered. I detect no energy at all. If I knew no better, I would swear we are not the same."

She was right. I was nothing like her. A few days ago I would have been happy to watch a creature like her die but having had my own body tied to a stake ready for burning had altered my views a little. She was still a witch though and everyone knows what witches do, don't they? Oh but there was Cain too... yet my brother was different. I knew he was.

"Sophie, please. We don't want to be rude and compel you

to show us your talent. Trust us. We saved you. What more proof do you require?"

"Nothing. I can't do anything." I'd had enough. Why would I want to talk to these witches? I had to get away, make sure Cain was safe.

I leapt to my feet and ran. They didn't attempt to stop me. Reaching the mouth of the cave I stood on a narrow rock shelf and stared out over a wide expanse of ocean. This was not my home.

"Where am I?"

"As long as you're among your own kind what difference does it make?"

I returned to the chair. "Please take me back. I don't have any magic. They made a mistake when they accused me of witchcraft. It does happen."

Hazel pouted. "Don't be ridiculous. If you couldn't do anything, why would they think you could? Do stop wasting our time. Oh, enough!" She reached out and her fingertips brushed my lips. "Tell me!"

I couldn't stop talking. I told them everything. "It wasn't me. It was my brother, Cain. I let them think I did it so they would take me and not him." Tears mingled with my words of betrayal.

"Where is he now?" She grasped my wrist and again a gentle warmth spread through me. "We want to help. You've done well to protect him but you can't save him. We can. Where is he?"

I told them. I described the mill by the race. I imagined him hiding inside and I told them what I saw.

Hazel nodded. "Good. Now some landmark, child. We go this minute."

Again the words fell from my lips. I could keep no secrets from these women. I admitted I was afraid of witches and they laughed, the sound merging with the gurgling of the mill stream. The cave was gone...

...and I was home.

The second witch questioned me and I responded. Cain and I worked all day in this mill for my elder brother and his greedy wife. A week ago we had all been together. Lucas fed the hopper on the floor above while Jayne made us drag the heavy grain sacks up to him. Cain stamped his foot and the next instant one of the sacks was in the air emptying itself over Jayne's head. Caught in a mottled brown and grey snow-storm, a blizzard of flying flour, she screamed and fled the mill, trailing the powder behind her.

Lucas gazed down, his mouth gaping open. "What have you done?"

We didn't have long to wait for the answer. She returned with several of our neighbours. I tried to convince them the sack had fallen from the floor above. When I saw they weren't going to believe me I told them I had caused the chaos. Lucas, who had seen everything, said nothing.

I was dragged away and tried as a witch but it was all a waste of time. Jayne's accusation was more than enough to condemn me.

The witches had learnt enough. The compulsion to talk was gone.

I led them inside. There was no-one in sight. The mill race gurgled but the wheel was held still. I wondered whether Lucas was at the burning, witnessing what he thought was my death. I shivered.

"Sophie! You're safe. Oh, Sophie!" Cain raced out from

between the sacks of grain. His stick thin arms locked around me. "I was so frightened. I thought you were dead."

"Is this the boy?"

I looked over his shoulder at the witch in the blue dress. "Yes, this is Cain."

He released me. His eyes were wide. "Who are these ladies? Did they save you?"

"Yes and, Cain, they're like you."

Hazel extended her hand. A cake appeared on her palm. "Are you hungry, Master Cain?"

"Are you a witch?" He was more fascinated than afraid.

"I am a sorceress and I hope you are going to be a sorcerer."

He took the cake. "Thank you. I can do things like that too."

"You're welcome. Now, would you like to show me what you can do?"

I tried to protest but she waved her fingers and I couldn't move.

Cain hadn't noticed anything was wrong. He was too busy. He opened his hand and there was Lucas' coin bag, the one he hangs from his belt. "Not bad, eh?"

"That's good but we will teach you to do so much more." Hazel chuckled. "It's time we were gone."

The second witch shook her head. "Wait. What about the girl? Oughtn't we to reward her?"

"She already has been. We rescued her from the flames. What more could she ask of us?"

"We can't leave her like this. They'll just carry her back to the fire. You're not being fair, Hazel. She risked her life for one of our kind."

"You're too soft. We have enough to do as it is."

"Perhaps but I still hold we can't reward her service to one of us by letting them burn her."

"We can't take her with us." Hazel grasped Cain's wrist but he kicked out at her.

"No! I won't go anywhere without Sophie."

Hazel tutted, twirled her hand and my brother fell senseless to the floor. She waved at me and I was free. "My sister is correct to reprimand me. You do deserve something. What is your wish? Money, jewellery...?"

"I don't want your money. I wish for my brother to stay with me."

She snorted. "Don't be silly. Haven't you any sensible requests?"

"You can't give me anything I want. I'll follow you wherever you take him. I will rescue him. You'd have to turn me to stone before I'd accept what you're doing."

She touched her fingers together. A faint blue light surrounded the tips. "That's your last word, is it? You would rather be a statue forever than lose your brother?"

I was so angry I didn't see the danger, not even when she smiled.

"In that case..." Her hand was in the air...

...and we were no longer in the mill. We were in the village square. I felt dizzy, disorientated, close to sleep.

"What about there?" She wasn't talking to me.

The second witch shrugged. "It's as good as anywhere, I suppose... but, Hazel, are you sure this is fair?"

"You heard the girl." Hazel's fingers ruffled my hair. "She'll be so pretty. People will come from all around to look."

She nodded to herself then smiled at me. "Nice. You will be much admired. Now, farewell."

She was gone. They were all gone, Cain with them.

————

I stand in the shallow bowl of the village fountain. I can't move my eyes but from their corners I see my arms are raised to the height of my shoulders. My hands are open and in each one sits a smaller stone bowl. I gaze straight ahead. My feet are in the water but there is no discomfort. There is nothing. I know if I could see myself, I would see the statue of a young girl.

Look upon me, friends, and learn of the unkindness of witches. Not for me a quick death by fire but instead a slow erosion of stone by weather, wind and water.

Could any nightmare be worse than this?

# THE KABUL INTERNATIONAL ROSE FESTIVAL

## PENNY ROGERS

---

*If you want to see god, give a gift of a rose to your neighbour.*
*Qur'an.*

---

It was Adnan's idea to hold a rose growing competition. When the British left Kabul in a hurry he didn't for one minute believe their promises that all Embassy staff would be safe. He supposed that they had good intentions, but the British government's good intentions usually got you nowhere unless you were very senior, and rarely extended to rank and file gardeners. He had worked there for almost two decades, keeping the lawns, flower beds, trees and shrubs in tip-top condition. He had hoped that he'd stay there forever but it all changed very quickly when the US pulled out of Afghanistan, and their British allies (or lap dogs depending on your point of view, thought Adnan) left with them.

With no work, and fearful to leave his compound unless

absolutely necessary, Adnan concentrated on the small garden in the corner of his yard. In it he grew his beloved roses; the plants had been given to him over the years as thank you tokens by successive Embassy officials and attachés. He had treasured these gifts; nurtured and propagated them, kept the plants as free as possible from black spot and other pests, delighting in the fragrance and beauty of each bloom.

———

The Taliban takeover had generally been less destructive than the chaos when the Mujahidin took control in 1989, but Adnan knew how precarious his situation was. The area commanders were rounding up dissidents and known western sympathisers, and as a long-time employee of the British he was vulnerable.

'So, how will you organise this festival?' Tariq was interested. Inspired by his older brother he also grew roses, although his work as a road mender had provided much less opportunity to perfect his skills.

'We'll start off small, just you and me. We'll do it like they do it at the Embassy. I'll tell Ayesha to make some sweets and we can judge each other's roses.'

'You're bound to win,' Tariq felt that the outcome was a foregone conclusion.

'We can't involve anyone else, not at the moment. Maybe next year.' Adnan looked around, terrified of eavesdroppers and spies. 'It might be safer' he carried on without much conviction 'Yes, it might be safer and we can ask everyone who grows roses to join in. And we'll get an outside judge. And have a prize.'

Tariq warmed to his brother's enthusiasm 'We could call it the Kabul International Rose Festival and some reporters might put us on CNN or the BBC. Al Jazeera might be really keen.'

'It might be stretching it a bit to call it *International*.' Adnan was always cautious.

'But it is' his brother countered 'our grandfather came from Uzbekistan so we are really Uzbeks, your Ayesha was born in Pakistan, our mother was a refugee from Iran. We are international.'

'Ok, I get your point but let's not get carried away, it might take a while before...' Adnan hesitated, choosing his words carefully, '...our *friends and brothers* think that's a good idea. Right now the only prize we'd get is a horrible death.' He shuddered and stroked his beard thoughtfully 'but we can have a small festival to start off with.'

———

In spite of the poor soil, scarcity of water and lack of fertilisers, roses grew surprisingly well in these tiny gardens. Both men favoured scented roses; Adnan's favourite was 'Compassion' with apricot-pink flowers against dark green leaves. It had been given to him many years ago by the wife of the ambassador. She had seen him tending the roses and been impressed by his care and skill, and when she left Kabul she gave him a plant in a plastic pot. He had never been given a gift by a woman outside of his family and he was embarrassed and confused by the gesture. Reluctantly he had taken it home and asked Ayesha what he should do. 'Plant it' she had said in her usual matter of fact manner, 'plant it and look after it.'

Tariq only had a few rose bushes. Mostly they were duplicates or cuttings from Adnan's collection. However, he did have a beautiful dark red rose called 'Royal William' that he had been given by a photographer who he'd helped set up a shoot for National Geographic. The shoot had involved keeping a space outside the Eid Gah Mosque clear of beggars, onlookers, kids and stray dogs for half an hour while photographs were taken. For some reason that Tariq never comprehended, this red rose was the focus of most of the shots. Anyway, when it was all over the photographer gave him $10 as agreed and the rose.

So 'Royal William' was Tariq's best hope of competing with his brother and he devoted as much time as possible to its care. The children were warned to stay away from the roses on pain of a good thrashing and he confiscated their football until the competition was over.

The date of the festival had yet to be decided. Adnan and Tariq wanted to get on with it; their delicate rose blooms did not last long in the hot, dusty air. But Ayesha was strangely hesitant.

'It is very difficult for me to get all the ingredients I need to make the sweetmeats.'

Adnan could see her point. She could not go shopping without a related male escort and he was afraid to go out in case he was recognised. Their son Farouk was seventeen and a willing escort, but he was at university studying to be an engineer, and like his father he didn't want to be seen on the street in case the Taliban rounded him up as a 'conscript'. But for some reason Ayesha would not even ask Farouk, or any of her other male relations, she just promised she'd go shopping as soon as possible. Meanwhile the roses were rapidly going past their best.

Finally a date was decided. It was to be the following Thursday. The shopping would be done on the Tuesday; Ayesha's cousin Ibrahim worked at the Pakistan Embassy and he said he would be pleased to escort her to go shopping. This suited Adnan very well; he enjoyed Ibrahim's company and he looked forward to talking to him over a few glasses of tea once the shopping had been done. This would enable Ayesha to do the cooking on the Wednesday in preparation for the grand event on the Thursday. Farouk had found an old silver cup in the bazaar and had inscribed it using an engraving tool he'd discovered in the workroom at the university. It proudly said 'Kabul International Rose Festival Champion Prize' in rather wonky script around the widest part of the cup.

Adnan proudly showed the trophy to Ibrahim as they sipped milky sheer chai, redolent with cinnamon, cardamom and saffron. 'So what is the news that I should know about?' He was anxious to hear what was going on, whether the Taliban were meeting any resistance and most importantly, what were the British doing about evacuating him.

Ibrahim was non-committal, 'There's nothing I know, we must all keep our heads down. And enjoy this splendid tea. Tell me more about your rose festival?' He picked up the cup and did his best to decipher the crude inscription.

On Wednesday Adnan was too busy with his roses to notice that Ayesha wasn't doing any food preparation. She was busy indoors as was usual, but he was too preoccupied to notice that her many activities did not extend to making sugar syrup, grinding spices and chopping nuts and dried fruit. It was getting dark when she came out to speak to him. 'We must go now; some transport will be here at 8.30. It will take us to Karachi, we will not come back.'

Adnan was too stunned to speak. He looked at his meek and compliant wife; had she gone mad? In the darkening evening she explained that the British had arranged the evacuation of him and his immediate family. He had not been told in case he had been rounded up; all the arrangements had been made by Ibrahim. The real reasons for the shopping expedition on Tuesday became clear; Adnan looked at the papers that his wife handed to him. They were for Adnan, Ayesha, Farouk and his two sisters.

'What about Tariq?' Adnan's relief was quickly replaced by fear for his brother and for his brother's family. 'I can't just leave them. What if the area commander realises I've gone. They might come for Tariq. If they do they'll torture him, kill him, and murder the kids, just because of me. I can't do this.'

'We must go. It is our only chance.' Ayesha was calm but adamant. 'When we are safe we can try to get visas for Tariq. If we stay none of us will ever be safe.'

'I must at least speak to him, explain what is happening.'

'NO!' Ayesha shouted at her husband for the first and only time. 'No. If he knows nothing he can tell them nothing. It is the safest way. The only way.'

———

By eight o'clock the bags packed by Ayesha were by the door. Adnan wanted to at least tell his brother that 'Royal William' was the winner of the first Kabul International Rose Festival, and beg him to stay safe. But Ayesha stood firm. 'The less Tariq knows the safer it will be for him.'

'You go' Adnan begged his wife. 'You go, take the children and I'll stay here. I'll keep out of the way; look after everything until you can return.'

'No you must come. Sooner or later they will come for you. They won't leave you much longer to grow roses. And think about Farouk, he will be conscripted. We'll never see him again.'

Adnan knew she was right. He was terrified for Farouk but also worried about Ayesha, no longer permitted to go about her daily activities, and his daughters who were forbidden to attend school. He consoled himself with the prospect of getting a job in Queen Elizabeth's garden, of Farouk working for Rolls Royce and his girls getting an education and good jobs. All would be well. Allahu Akbar.

————

Six months later a battered package was delivered to Tariq. The hurt he had felt at being left behind was still raw; as he saw it, his brother had abandoned him for a better life in the UK and had not even had the decency to tell him that he was leaving. He no longer cared about his roses; he had given up on them and left them to struggle, forsaken just as he had been. He looked at the package with distrust. What if it contained explosives? In the end he took it outside to open it, reasoning that it must have been checked many times before it had been delivered to him.

Inside the package he found the cup. His eyes grew misty

as he read the proud words etched around it. As well as the cup there was a letter and a postcard of a rose, a red rose. He wasn't at all sure that it was 'Royal William', but that didn't matter. Tariq went indoors and put the cup in the centre of the one low table. Later he might go out and tend his roses, after he had read Adnan's letter.

# THE ALTERNATIVE 800 METRES

PAUL SHERMAN

From his small bedroom window, Abraham could only see his beloved aerodrome, a mass of concrete and a decrepit runway but Abraham loved it nonetheless… especially the runway… his racetrack… his Olympia.

The high-rise block of flats stood at the edge of the derelict aerodrome. From his bedroom window, Abraham Nguru was spared the view of the other high rises and the sprawling mess that was the inner city, with its tawdry playgrounds awash with graffiti, the bleak comprehensive school with its single lung of a playing field, avenues of bumper-to-bumper slow-moving traffic, the depressing mist hanging lower than the tops of the tower blocks. He had worked hard clearing it. Much of the debris he had moved himself. But two of his school buddies had helped him shift the larger blocks. He'd saved hard-earned money from his part-time supermarket job to buy a rake, with which he had smoothed the rubble on the runway, leaving the surface level enough for his running.

Abraham loved to run. He ran as it his life depended upon

it. At five-thirty in the morning, Abraham would make his mother a cup of tea and take it to her so she could drink it in bed. He checked she had everything she needed, the gas fire on if it was cold, the radio tuned to Radio 4, then he would say:

"Just goin' running Mum."

"Take care Abe," she'd caution, looking in his direction with sightless eyes.

"Will do," he'd assure her and then he would sprint down the twenty flights of stairs, avoiding the lift, to step out on to the front patio of the tower block.

It was five hundred yards to the runway he had so lovingly nurtured for two months, and which now resembled an Olympic racetrack… exactly what Abraham intended. He knelt down, gathered the fine dust in his hands and then let it slide through his fingers.

"You're good," he told the earth.

The track wasn't oval or circular like the real thing. It was wide enough to give him room to turn after the first 400 metres, although he still had to angle quite sharply to run the final 400 metres back. But it did the job. He had marked out the start post and finishing post with oil drums. The start line was a row of pebbles and the finish line was a length of string tied between two oil drums.

Abraham became an Olympic fantasist. He knelt in his affordable middle-of-the-range running shoes, and waited for the imaginary pistol shot. When it burst upon the morning aerodrome air, Abraham ran. This was when he felt life was for living. Heart full pelt, limbs toned, cold morning air invigorating his face, blood singing in his veins, triumph whistling in his ears, the imaginary roar of the crowd urging him to glory, he *knew*, as he crossed the finish line, arms held high, that he was worthy of being an Olympic champion. Oh yes, Abraham Nguru could win Gold. For his country. For Great Britain.

Later he cooked breakfast for his Mum… two soft boiled eggs with brown bread and butter, served up with a mug of hot sweet tea.

"You's a good boy, Abe," she said warmly, "You enjoy your run today?"

"Yes, Mum," he said, the words inadequate to describe his elated sensation of fulfilment. He wanted his mother to *know* his feelings; when the time was right, he would share his greatest moment with her. She would be so proud of him.

He would stand on a pedestal for her and the gold medal would sit on the mantelpiece.

Although she wouldn't see it, she would pick it up and feel it and remember that eventful day in June 2012.

Mr Wakeling, the PE teacher at Grove Comprehensive, championed Abraham.

"Come on, lad," he'd say, "You've got talent. You're fit, you're fast and you could outrun champions. But you've got to be focussed. You've got to run like you really want to win. You've got to see that golden pillar in the clouds. And you run towards it. Grasp it. You leap into the sky and come out the other side. When your heart feels like it's going to burst and the lactic acid in your muscles is making them scream, *that's* when you start really trying. That's what champions are made of, lad."

When he'd finished talking, there was a film of perspiration on his brow. It was as if Mr Wakeling himself was leaping through the mist, reaching for that golden pillar.

Abraham won most of the school sports day running events and many inter-school contests, also competing for the City Under-Eighteens. He'd been offered a national training course, but couldn't afford the fee. The school couldn't cough up and his dad never answered his letters in which Abraham tried to find out if he could sponsor him.

"It's a diabolical tragedy, lad," Mr Wakeling told him, "It's a crying-out-loud shame. If I had the money, which on my salary, I don't, I'd give it you meself."

Although disappointed, Abraham knew the man bitterly resented that he couldn't help.

"However," Mr Wakeling went on, "There'll be folk out there looking for talent. Scouts. You need to be discovered lad. That's how it works. I've got contacts. But I'm not saying it's a certainty, mind."

Abraham knew there was little chance… which was why he felt impelled to stage his own personal event, with his mother present to hear, if at least not see, his victory.

Abraham took her out often. It was a struggle to get her into her wheelchair, get the wheelchair out of the flat and into the lift, but Abraham achieved it with the true devotion of a loving son.

Sometimes he wheeled her to the school playing field, took her around the perimeter, describing some of the times he had won races and been presented with the trophies that he'd taken home for her. At other times, he'd take her to the aerodrome; she loved to be there on a crisp day when the breeze straddled the airfield and tugged at her curls.

"This is where I'm gonna make you proud of me, mum," he said.

"I'm already proud of you, Abe," she responded, her

fingers squeezing his hand which rested lightly on her shoulder. Abraham didn't see the tears in her eyes, but he felt the warmth of her words.

Abe's heart was bursting. She was going to be there when he won Olympic Gold.

That day dawned bright and clear. When he got up, he checked the aerodrome out of the widow. The track looked perfect. He couldn't wait for ten o'clock and the 800 metres final. On the table were his 'props'. His portable CD player/radio, loaded with new batteries, his medal that he'd lovingly forged in the school metalwork shop and then adorned with gold paint and a red ribbon, the CD of 'UK Patriotic Tunes' …and finally, a stopwatch, borrowed from school.

"I don't know what you doing boy, but I feel somthin' is happenin'." This as he wheeled her down in the graffiti-ridden litter-infested lift, carrying all his 'props' on the handle of the wheelchair.

"What you up to? I never seen you like this befo'…" This as he secured the brake on her wheelchair at the side of the track… by the starting line and the finishing line that lay side by side on the disused runway.

""'S okay, Mamma," he said. "I won't be far away, don't worry. This day you gonna be real proud of me."

He placed the radio-CD player by her chair, turned it on and quickly tuned it in to Five Live.

It was the build-up the final… the 800 metres. The commentators were in fine fettle and the excited roar of the crowd was unmistakeable. The competitors were lining up.

Line up, Abraham's inner voice told him. You've been training for this. Do it!

He took his position on his home-made starting line as he'd done many times before. Heart racing, he awaited the starter's orders.

Bang!

They were off.

He had to get into his pace in the first 200 metres (Wakey-Wakey had taught him this). He mustn't slow down. When he reached 400 metres, he should feel tired but relaxed. He found the energy to accelerate into the 500-metre stretch. With 300 to go, he had to keep the pressure on the gas pedal.

Into the final 150 and it felt like an elephant had jumped onto his calf muscles as the lactic acid took control.

He was near the finishing line; the roar of the crowd was in his ears. He was ahead. His competitors were nowhere to be seen. He hadn't slowed. He'd won the race. Abraham burst through the string, hands raised. He finished with a circular jog towards him Mum and knelt down beside her, gasping as if his lungs would burst.

"Listen, Mum," he managed to say.

The winner's time was announced. Abraham opened his hand where he'd been clutching the stop watch. He had clicked it on the finishing line.

"Mum," he whispered in excitement, "I beat the Gold Medal Olympic runner's time. I'm a champion, Mamma."

He flicked off the radio and set the CD to play 'God Save the Queen.' He stood proudly and placed his school-made gold medal around his neck.

"I done this for my country," he announced. Then he knelt

by his mother again and whispered the words again "I done this for my country, Mamma."

He placed the gold medal in her palm, enclosing her fingers around it.

"Feel it, Mamma," he urged her. "I know you can't see, but it's gold. *Gold!*"

She put her arms around Abraham's neck, clutching the medal and told him, "My beautiful son. I'll never stop being proud of you, boy."

Was it time for Abraham to say "I know it's only make-believe Mum."?

No, with their tears flowing and mingling, there was no need.

No need for any further words.

# PHOENIX

## BRYAN THOMAS

One surprisingly hot, sultry June evening, after a tiring day of culture, looking at Wren churches, I was wandering, somewhat aimlessly, around the older streets of Bow in East London when I came across a small pub.

—

The Phoenician was one of those dark old inns; brown mahogany tables and blackened low beams. The walls were hung with 'Old London' prints, and a row of pewter mugs lined a high shelf. Worn old quarry tiles covered the floor, and the smell of slightly warm beer hung over all. There was a quiet murmur of voices, and the only empty pew was in a dim recess where an elderly man was hunched, sipping a pint.

He had gnarled old hands. His knuckles looked stiff, and his fist gripped the tall glass of ale with a fierce intensity as he raised it, a little shakily, to his lips. As we started chatting, he told me he had been a monumental mason and worked on several Wren churches before retiring. On learning about my studies, he mentioned a recurring dream that had puzzled him over recent months.

"It goes something like this," he began. "I'm in this bloody great underground cavern workin' by the light of sputterin' torches hung on the walls all around. I am there, carvin' inscriptions and figures on these sarcophaguses – like coffins for dead folks," he explains. "It's bloody hard work because the stone is granite, the tools are funny and not very sharp, but I have the knack for it. The carvin' is sort of realistic- like, with goats 'n cows in a land what looks bloody hot and tells the story of ordinary-looking folks. With their heads at funny angles, the tall figures are like marchin' up an' down with long poles, some of 'em with eagles an' such on top and with chickens scratchin' away under their feet."

"Some days, my supervisor lets me carve the creatures that will go along with the dead. The sandstone is easier to work with. It's sort of artistic; gives me a buzz, kind of, when the birds an' animals look real".

"If you don't mind the stink of them torches an' the piss an' sweat down here, the work is great. More'n you can say for the poor buggers I hear about, beaverin' away on the outside in the heat and dust. They are grindin' the faces of the great blocks an', when they are done, they 'ave to break their backs haulin' them into place, day after day, month after month. Then, if they get ill with a fever or if the liftin' finally does for them, they are pitched down the long slopes to die an' get to feed the bloody vultures. Rather be down here, I tell myself and stay out o' bleedin' trouble".

———

The old man takes a long draught then grins up at me to see if I am still listening. "Keep going", I say, fetching him another pint.

"In my dream, I hear a rumour, one time," he goes on, "that the Pharaoh is dyin' and that this place, after the hoo-ha an' the praying stuff, must be ready to bury him."

"There are soldiers now, and supervisor guys, an' more people are workin' down here than ever. They are layin' out long rows of empty bowls an' jugs, rings 'n bangles an' even, like robes and headdresses."

———

It is being rumoured that we will not be let free, even when the job is finished. Maybe a load of rubbish, but it gets me worried.

———

"I never seen anyone leave for the outside and, after talkin' to several of me mates when the guards' backs are turned, I begin to think that the rumours are true. So when the soldiers are pissed 'an sleepin' it off, I sneak away to a dark corner behind a pile of stone rubble and do a special bit of carving of my own."

"Soon, there are loads of great chests bein' moved in an'

jars of all bloody shapes an' sizes; the little'ns for herbs an' spices; the bigger ones are full of corn an' oils. Some jars are full of wine, and when I get the chance, I take a long swig or two. Well, mate, got to keep my own ruddy spirits up, ain't I?"

"Well," I reply, looking up at the ceiling, " I think you had better stick to that principle. Another pint ?"

"Don't mind if I do. Join me, and I'll carry on."

———

I returned with the drinks, and I asked him to continue. We clinked glasses, and I stared at the ceiling, wondering where this was all going. His story seemed incredibly detailed, and he was not the sort of chap one would expect to have the confidence or the stamina to do the amount of research which would clearly be needed. I came back to earth.

"One day, we hear the fuckin' truth. We **are** goin' to be buried with the great King, to be 'is slaves, when they say, we will all be 'resurrected'. The animals an' birds that we've carved will wake up as well. The grub 'n wine has been stored, ready for us in the next world."

"The bloody cup final comes at last an', with a load of poncey malarkey, the

blowin' of horns an' the blood of sacrifices pourin' into the cracked stone floors. Ramses, bloody II is laid to rest. A great stone is rolled across the last opening to the outside. Quite soon, the last torch splutters an' goes out. Then, in the scary dark, some stupid bugger kicks over the last pitcher of water, and the wailin' begins.

· · · · ·

"Time to go, I say to meself. I haven't worked for forty years to be buried with some bloody trumped-up Pharaoh."

"I feel me way around the walls until I reach the special place – me spare time work is about to pay off. Pushin' hard on the keystone I'd carved, I open up the last ventilation shaft, squeeze in an' push it softly shut behind me. Over the last few weeks, I have lifted quite a few bits' n' bobs out of the chests, so draggin' me sack full of jools behind me, I start crawlin' towards the dim glow at the end of the tunnel…"

He pauses again, and seeing that I am not yet ready to give him a refill, he continues.

"I promise meself that I will soon be havin' a great time watchin' the kids splash about in the river, and I might even empty the sand out of my old felucca an' do a bit of sailin' like when I was a lad. Only then it hits me; I know the way out, so I can pop back any time if the coffers are getting' a tad low."

He pauses; "That's me dream then. I suppose the archaeology stuff is a load of bollocks, but the stink an' the carvin' and such make it all feel so bloody real." He drains his glass, pauses and then suggests his own answer to the puzzle.

"Is my dream some sort of inherited memory?" he asks cautiously, as though he had learnt the phrase by heart. "I heard tell that one of me ancestors was a freed slave in the Roman army which finished up in London. Us Cockneys go back a hell of a long way, and our Pearly Kings 'n Queens must've got their loot from somewhere, know what I mean?"

He leans back and looks at me quizzically, then muttering

about takin' a leak, he clambers unsteadily to his feet, raising a sinewy arm in salutation. Behind the yellowing, grey beard, he has a deeply tanned face, unlikely in a true East Londoner. His sandaled feet are bare, and is there just a hint of a gelabi from somewhere way back in his baggy, tattered, white trousers and long, white cotton shirt?

He does not return, and the pub is quieter as I make my way past the bar. The Landlord stops polishing the brass and says, " I see you've been chatting to Fred. With his white outfit and his sandals, I bet he's been telling you about his work on the Pyramids."

"He told me his dream," I say.

"He's a rare one," says the Landlord. "In winter, he would have dressed in sea boots, with a long blue coat complete with epaulettes and gold buttons, to tell you his dream about the Armada. Of being the Captain of a Spanish Galleon – the only survivor washed ashore, nearly drowned and being looked after by an English village lass.

"Or with a multi-coloured coat, a stiff leg and an eye patch recounting his adventures as a pirate in the Caribbean. Of being captured and locked up in the Tower of London awaiting death, until a servant girl helped him to escape through the tunnels.

"Very good for business is our Fred," says mine host, returning to his polishing. Mind how you go. It's hot out there."

The whiff from the toilets and the reflections in the polished brass from the sputtering of electric wall candles behind the bar turn my mind back to the old man's dream world in the monster cavern.

I open the heavy oak door to feel the heat and a draft of hot air picking up the sand and have to shut my eyes against the glare. When I open them, all I can see is an endless desert with the tracks left by a small bent figure heading towards a distant pyramid in the mirage. On a zephyr, I catch the echo of a wheezy chuckle.

# I HOPE THIS FINDS YOU WELL

RICHARD WESTWELL

Sir,

I hope this letter finds you well.

Please disregard for a moment your most unusual present circumstances; all will be explained very shortly. You will find a small bottle of water at your left elbow; I encourage you to take as much as you need. We anticipate that your mouth will be dry. It is unclear how much comprehension of the recent ceremony you will have, but it is our hope that your situation now is at least comfortable. The light by which you are reading this letter comes from a small battery-powered lantern behind your head, the lifespan of which should be perfectly adequate for our purposes.

You will have some pressing questions, which I will do my best to answer briefly. These are likely to centre on the matters of where you are and how you got there. For reasons which will become clear, I will start by answering the second of these enquiries.

You have done, you will agree, a tremendous quantity of

evil in your life to date. You have inflicted great cruelty upon your wife and children, and both physical and financial harm not only to your rivals but also to those who once called you a friend. No, do not get angry. The narcotics which were administered to you yesterday evening are only now beginning to dissipate, and an increase in heart rate is most inadvisable. Instead, use this moment of tranquillity, lying there in the flickering shadows, to reflect upon what you know to be true – you have been a deeply bad person.

It is fitting to mention whence came the design to sedate you for the purpose of punishment. Fitting because your wife made the acquaintance of our village apothecary after several trips to his establishment to purchase dressings and salves for the injuries you enacted upon her. This is an irony that you can surely appreciate.

I know this apothecary to be of excellent character, being his brother. My own wife laughs at the thought of how many customers he might contrive to send me if he were only a little less fastidious with his weights and measures, but in reality he has never before taken action of this sort, you may rest assured.

It is quite understandable that you are not in a position to reply to this communication, and no reply is expected. As I write, word has come from your wife that you have devoured every morsel of the drugged pudding she prepared and are already coiled in the snoring embrace of Morpheus. When I have finished this missive, I will put it unsealed into the envelope you will have found placed on your chest, as I do not expect a man buried under six feet of fresh earth to be in possession of a letter-opener.

I am certain that you now appreciate that in the act of

explaining *why* you are in your current position, I have also answered the *where*. Yes, you have been **buried alive**, and are reading this from a recumbent attitude inside one of my finest mahogany coffins (for as you will have guessed, I am the undertaker of this parish).

Now, sir – your excellent wife does not wish these tidings to bring you to total despair, so it is most important to confirm immediately that your interment is only a temporary state of affairs, designed to demonstrate to you the pain that duress and the abuse of power may bring. *To teach you a lesson*, in other words, a lesson which you will be unable to curtail or resist, being quite literally a captive audience. Rage all you want; **you will remain in your coffin until Monday morning,** when you will be liberated in, we hope, a chastened and more reasonable state of mind.

Your funeral service was a quiet family affair, with only a few carefully invited acquaintances who wished to be present at the moment of your downfall. You are a short man in the largest coffin available, which caused eyebrows to raise until we explained the necessity of providing a sufficient initial supply of oxygen. Given my profession, the preacher is a close confidant, so there was no need for alarm when an urgent knocking began to issue from your casket – on the contrary this merely encouraged us to sing *Jerusalem* all the louder.

We perceive that your immediate concern will be this quantity of breathable air, but there you need have no fear. Discreet rubber tubes have been linked to small holes drilled into the base of your coffin – you may be able to see them in the dimming light if you twist your legs – and the cemetery caretaker, old Bowker, has been instructed to attend your graveside every eight hours, rain or shine, there to work the small foot pump concealed beneath the cast-iron flower holder. In this way the oxygen may be replenished regularly, leaving you in relative comfort until your forthcoming deliverance.

In summary, you have been buried alive to teach you a much-needed lesson about humanity, and you will remain so buried for two full days. With this understanding, it is our sincere hope that you will have by now returned to a state of calm and have recovered fully from what must have been a most unpleasant initial shock.

It is probable that you are recuperated to the point of confident wrath and are even now plotting some violent revenge against those friends and family who have reduced you to your present condition.

Which brings us to our ultimate point, and the final page of this communication. Please, have a drink from your water bottle – you have ample to last two days, and it would be a shame for you to spill any once the battery for your lantern expires.

Is your thirst slaked? Then it is with some gratification that we wish at last to apprise you of the fact that we have not been altogether *honest* hitherto.

One can only plumb the depths of misery after first raising oneself to the heights of great hope, do you agree? It was your wife's concern that the very fact of waking up in your own coffin might provoke in you a feeling of numbed fatalism, quite at odds with the stabbing pain of anguish she wished you to experience. And so, it is now our pleasant duty to inform you that the hope of release and revenge given to you by this communication thus far was a fiction, designed to raise your spirits the better to dash them now onto the rocks of despair.

**To be clear – we are *not* going to free you**. *No one is going to dig you out.* You *do* have the air supply mentioned above, but only because we consider death by thirst a more agonisingly slow way to die than mere suffocation. The lantern's battery will soon expire, leaving you to suffer parched misery in the cruel dark alone.

Please be aware that any cries or screams from your direction will be deadened long before reaching the surface. It is possible that some sound may travel up by way of your breathing tubes, but the narrowness of this passage will produce only the thin moaning redolent of an unhappy wind, quite appropriate for a lonely country graveyard.

A last word from myself in a more business-like vein. In order to offer my services as cheaply as possible to your deserving wife it is my desire to disinter this fine wooden coffin for reuse in a month or two (long after your passing, no matter how protracted), and I would therefore be most grateful if you could refrain from scratching at the inside of the lid with your fingernails. I can assure you of the futility of this, as the wood is an inch thick and nailed down most securely.

Rest assured that your family and friends are thinking of you at this time.

I remain, sir, your most obedient servant.

# ACKNOWLEDGMENTS

This is the first Henshaw Press Short Story anthology that we have published so we can't claim much credit for this venture. For that, we would like to express our heartfelt thanks to Graham Jennings, who has overseen the Henshaw Press competition since its inception and who has entrusted us with the baton from May 2023 onwards. We really hope we can do you proud, Graham, and keep up your excellent work.

We'd also like to thank all the judges of the competition, who give their time freely and willingly.

Thanks also to Victoria Dowd for her beautifully written Foreword to this book and for her support and encouragement. It's good to know that there are people out there who love short stories as much as we do!

We can't not thank the extremely talented writers who have contributed to this anthology. Thank you, everyone, firstly, for entering the Henshaw Press Short Story competition in the first place. Secondly, thank you for winning a prize. Finally, thank you for allowing us to publish your stories in this book. Without you, this book wouldn't exist.

Thanks also to Julia Edwards of the Christopher Whitehead Language College and Sixth Form, Worcester. We were so thrilled that you approached us at just the right time and now your wonderful students are going to benefit from as many new books as we can buy from the profits from this anthology for their library, which for many is a refuge from the harsh realities of life but, more importantly, is a portal to greater knowledge and imagined worlds.

Finally, thank you dear reader. If you have come across this book by chance and it intrigued you, then we thank you for taking a punt. We hope it has met your expectations, and more. Even better, perhaps it inspired you to write. If so, we know of a little competition you might like to enter…

REBECCA & ADRIAN
HOBECK BOOKS

# ABOUT HENSHAW PRESS

Henshaw Press is a small imprint that runs the four-times-a-year not-for-profit Henshaw Press Short Story Competition.

Henshaw Press was launched by a small group of writers, editors, lecturers and of course readers who wished to actively support creative writing. They ran quarterly competitions throughout the year with closing dates at the end of March, June, September and December.

The competition is still going strong, albeit under new management (Hobeck Books). The competition asks for original stories of up to 2,000 words on any subject, and is open to anyone over the age of sixteen. The fee for entry is just £6. For each competition there is a first prize award of £200, second prize of £100 and third prize of £50. The competition is open to anyone, anywhere, from any background.

If you are under sixteen, all is not lost, you can send your short story to Henshaw Press to get a free critique by an expert in the field.

Henshaw Press also offers critiques to competition entrants, for a fee of £14.

If you are interested in entering, please check the website www.henshawpress.co.uk for details.

All profits from the June 2023 competition and the publishing of this anthology will be used to purchase books for the school library at the Christopher Whitehead Language College and Sixth Form, Worcester, UK.

# HOBECK BOOKS – THE HOME OF GREAT STORIES

We hope you've enjoyed reading this anthology, which is published for the first time by Hobeck Books.

We offer a number of our authors' own short stories and novellas, free for subscribers in the compilation *Crime Bites*. Simply subscribe to www.hobeck.net to claim your free copy. As a subscriber, you will also receive our weekly newsletter plus updates on all our publishing news and competitions.

- *Echo Rock* by Robert Daws
- *Old Dogs, Old Tricks* by AB Morgan
- *The Silence of the Rabbit* by Wendy Turbin
- *Never Mind the Baubles: An Anthology of Twisted Winter Tales* by the Hobeck Team (including many of the Hobeck authors and Hobeck's two publishers)
- *The Clarice Cliff Vase* by Linda Huber
- *Here She Lies* by Kerena Swan
- *The Macnab Principle* by R.D. Nixon
- *Fatal Beginnings* by Brian Price
- *A Defining Moment* by Lin Le Versha
- *Saviour* by Jennie Ensor
- *You Can't Trust Anyone These Days* by Maureen Myant

Please visit the Hobeck Books website for details of our other superb authors and their books, and if you would like to get in touch, we would love to hear from you.

Hobeck Books also presents a weekly podcast, the Hobcast, where founders Adrian Hobart and Rebecca Collins discuss all things book related, key issues from each week, including the ups and downs of running a creative business. Each episode includes an interview with one of the people who make Hobeck possible: the editors, the authors, the cover designers. These are the people who help Hobeck bring great stories to life. Without them, Hobeck wouldn't exist. The Hobcast can be listened to from all the usual platforms but it can also be found on the Hobeck website: **www.hobeck.net/ hobcast**.

If you like short stories, Hobeck Books has also published two Christmas charity anthologies, which has be come an annual tradition now, *The Dark Side of Christmas* and *Cooking the Books.*

# UNLOCKED

From murder to magic, loss to love, Berlin to Bologna and everything in between, this brilliant anthology showcases 16 unique short stories from the **D20 Authors**, a best-selling group of writers whose debuts were published during the COVID 2020 lockdowns.

Meet the cleaner who won't let anything stand between her

and her job; the ocean diver with a mysterious mission; the pyromaniac driven by a painful compulsion; and the politician struggling to balance it all....

Compiled by best-selling author Philippa East, and covering everything from crime to romance, mystery to uplit, this multi-genre collection has a story for everyone. Contributors to *UnLocked* have been longlisted, shortlisted and winners of a variety of awards, including The Waterstones Children's Book Prize, The McIlvanney Prize for Best Scottish Crime Book, The Guardian's Not-The-Booker Prize, The People's Book Prize for Fiction, and the CWA New Dagger Award for best debut of the year.

With this superb anthology, the D20 Authors are delighted to be raising funds for the **Trussell Trust**, a charity who supports a nationwide network of food banks, and together they provide emergency food and support to people facing hardship, and campaign to end the need for food banks in the UK.

www.truselltrust.org

CPSIA information can be obtained
at www.ICGtesting.com
Printed in the USA
BVHW030357210623
666149BV00016B/1073